In A.D. 1212 a twelve-year-old shepherd boy, called
Stephen, went to King Philip of France with a letter
which he said came from Christ himself, bidding
Stephen organize a Crusade to rescue the holy city of
Jerusalem from the hands of the Infidel. In spite of the
King's disapproval, this strange boy announced that he
would lead this Crusade, and that it would be of
children.

Out of this inspiring and tragic piece of history Henry
Treece has conjured up a wonderful story. His hero and
heroine, Geoffrey and Alys de Villacours, may not have
existed in real life, but the suffering and hardships they
endured as they and thousands of other children
followed the young fanatic across France were real
enough. And so too was the terrible disillusionment at
Marseilles, when the sea refused to dry up for the young
Christians to cross, and instead evil men lured them on
to ships which did indeed go to the Holy Land, but
where the young victims were sold into slavery.

How Geoffrey and his sister were separated on that
dreadful journey, how they both became slaves to the
Governor of Egypt, and how they eventually made their
way home is told in this exciting book. For intelligent
readers of ten upwards.

Henry Treece was born in 1911. He was University
Boxing Captain and during the Second World War was
a Flight Lieutenant in Bomber Command. Besides
being a historical novelist, he wrote poetry and was a
critic, short-story writer, broadcaster and occasional
playwright. He was a lecturer on poetry at the Poetry
Center, New York, and the University of Buffalo, and
Theatre Correspondent for the Manchester Guardian.
Henry Treece died in 1966.

Some other Puffins by Henry Treece

HORNED HELMET
LEGIONS OF THE EAGLE
THE VIKING SAGA

THE CHILDREN'S CRUSADE

HENRY TREECE

ILLUSTRATED BY
CHRISTINE PRICE

PUFFIN BOOKS

Puffin Books, Penguin Books Ltd, Harmondsworth, Middlesex, England
Viking Penguin Inc., 40 West 23rd Street, New York, New York 10010, U.S.A.
Penguin Books Australia Ltd, Ringwood, Victoria, Australia
Penguin Books Canada Limited, 2801 John Street, Markham, Ontario, Canada L3R 1B4
Penguin Books (N.Z.) Ltd, 182–190 Wairau Road, Auckland 10, New Zealand

First published by The Bodley Head 1958
Published in Puffin Books 1964
Reprinted 1967, 1970, 1971, 1973, 1976, 1977, 1986

Printed and bound in Great Britain by
Hazell Watson & Viney Limited,
Member of the BPCC Group,
Aylesbury, Bucks
Set in Linotype Georgian

To

BARBARA KER WILSON

who suggested this theme

Contents

PART FOUR

PART FIVE

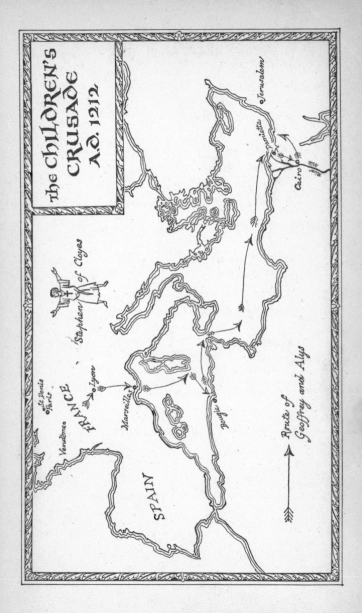

The Children's Crusade
A.D. 1212

St Denis
Paris
Vendôme
FRANCE

Stephen of Cloyes

Lyon

Marseilles

SPAIN

Bougie

Jerusalem

Damietta

Cairo
mouths of Nile

Route of
Geoffrey and Alys

PART ONE

*

1. *Lost Hawk*

THE great green hill of Saint Antoine stood hunched and
bristling with stout oaks in the early spring sunshine. Far
below, beside the shallow blue stream with its grey stone
bridge, lay the little castle of the Count Robert de Villacours
de la Franché. Above the hill stretched the immense blue
sky, broken here and there by bellying white clouds which
seemed for all the world as though they were themselves
monstrously battlemented fortresses of snow.

Here and there on the hillside sheep moved intently, their
new white lambs beside them, nibbling the sweet green
grass. A tousle-headed shepherd boy in a blue smock played
a catchy little tune on a pipe, jigging on his wooden pattens
in time to his melody as he followed the flock along.

Below, in the flat water-meadows by the stream, a herd of
sullen black cattle grazed quietly in the sunlight, flicking
their tails lazily to drive away the flies that were already
beginning to be troublesome as the day's heat increased.

To the south the distant hills of the Auvergne loomed
blue-grey in the spring sunshine. All seemed at peace – as
though there were no robbers and murderers in the whole
of France – no warring noblemen to ambush each other out
of jealousy and revenge – no ambushes, no battles, no
Crusades. ...

Suddenly, beyond the crown of the hill, this peace was
broken. A white dove swept down out of the blue sky, almost
as low as the clustered oaks, its wings beating in terror.
Above it poised the reason for this fear – a fully grown pere-
grine falcon, its broad wings flickering on the still air as it
took sight of its quarry before the swoop.

Given twenty seconds more, the dove might have reached the shelter of the oakwoods, where the low-hung branches, thick with leaves, would have afforded protection. ... But the hunted bird was allowed no such grace; the hawk was already in full career down the spring sky, its grey wings held so closely to its body that the bird resembled a viciously clenched fist holding a dagger, rather than a creature of feathered flight.

Yet even as the falcon's plunge carried it to within a lance's length of the terrified dove, there came a drumming of hooves from within the wood and a white palfrey appeared, lathered with haste, and bearing a young girl who waved her blue mantle furiously in her hand like a banner as she rode forward.

'Shoo, you brute!' she shouted, her golden hair fallen from its snood and flying behind her as she rode.

'Shoo! Shoo! Away with you, murderer!'

She flicked upward with the blue cloak, as her pony circled the turfy hollow beside the oakwood. The falcon seemed to halt with shock in his swoop, and with a violent fluttering of wing, narrowly avoided crashing to the ground.

The girl rode towards the hawk, swishing the mantle outwards violently. The bird of prey swept round, its cold eye glinting fiercely at her in the sunlight, then with a high-pitched scream of rage it swung above the trees.

'Hek-kek-kek-kek!' it cried as it disappeared.

The girl wiped her brows and smiled. The dove was nowhere to be seen, but at least it was not a mangled heap of bloodstained feathers on the grass, as it would have been had she arrived a moment later than she did.

'Good luck, Jeannine, my dove, my pretty!' she called. 'Stay in the wood till dusk and then come down to the cote in safety. I will bring you corn and broken bread in the morning, my pet!'

Then the smile left her face. There was a thundering of hooves behind her and she turned her pony to face the oncoming rider on the foaming black horse. He towered above her, his grey eyes blazing, his golden hair as tumbled as her own. On his left hand he wore the thick horsehide glove of a falconer; a bunch of coloured feathers swung at his gilded saddle-bow. In his right hand he held a riding-switch.

'Alys, you fool!' he shouted. 'You milksop idiot! I saw what you did to my best tiercel! And all for a worthless pigeon.'

The girl tried to smile at the boy. 'Brother Geoffrey,' she said haltingly, 'I could not help myself. But I could not stand by to see little Jeannine torn to pieces by that killer, could I?'

The boy's eyes blazed. He kicked so hard in his rage at the black horse's flanks that the creature, almost as angry as its master, reared and snorted, and almost charged the white palfrey, which now stood panting and shuddering with fright.

'Do you know what it is to train a hawk!' yelled the boy. 'Do you? Do you? If you had sat up with it, night after night, for weeks at a stretch, you would know how much I love it. If you had suffered its anger, its beak and its talons, as I have done, you would understand why I am furious! And after what you've done, the tiercel will never return. My hawk is lost for ever!'

Suddenly the girl's face changed. Her own fear left her and in its place came an expression of haughty disdain. She gazed up at the angry boy as though he were a petulant little child.

'There, there, *mon petit*,' she said, masking the fright that still made her heart flutter, 'you shall have another hawk! I will model you one out of clay – then it will not peck you, little brother! Nor will it fly away and leave you as this stupid creature has done!'

She could not have chosen more insulting words if she had thought hard for a week. The boy's mouth opened, as though he was about to say something that would wipe the girl from the face of the earth. But his fury made him dumb and no words would come.

Then, with a hoarse cry, he kicked at his mount and

raised the long riding-switch to strike the girl across the shoulders in his temper. She gazed at him in fear once more, but did not shrink from the blow.

Yet that blow never fell. The angry boy felt a sharp blow on the hand, and stared aghast at the heavy bull's hide whip-thong which encircled his wrist tightly. His own

riding-switch dropped from his imprisoned hand. He swung round in the saddle, groping with his left hand for his dagger, hampered by the thick hide falconer's glove.

'*Splendeur de Dieu!*' he exclaimed.

He faced another horseman, a man who seemed as broad as he was high, whose thick curly black hair hung over his swarthy forehead, whose thin black moustaches curled up almost until they touched his eyes, whose square black beard jutted forward arrogantly. Geoffrey noted that the man wore thin gold ear-rings, a worn leather tunic, with the rust-marks of chain-armour, and that a much dented iron helmet swung at his plain wooden saddle-bow.

Geoffrey dragged out the dagger with his left hand and kneed his horse round so as to slacken the tension on the whip-thong which held his right arm prisoner.

The black-haired man swung away from him then, sprawling the boy from the saddle with the violence of the sudden movement.

'*Mon dieu!*' he growled in a deep voice. 'But is there not enough fighting to do in the world but a boy must take a whip to a girl?'

His sneering lips, which bared to show his white teeth, were too much for Geoffrey's pride. He had never been spoken to before in this manner, and in the presence of his sister too!

The boy ran forward. 'I dare take a dagger to you, horse thief,' he shouted, and raised his hand.

The long lash streaked out again and the dagger flew away harmlessly into a clump of gorse at the wood's edge. Geoffrey stared ruefully after it, now almost in tears.

Then, collecting what dignity he still had, he controlled himself and said, 'Very well, my friend; you may think that you have scored over me now, but I give you this advice – turn your horse now and ride as fast as you can go, which will not be far by the sorry look of the animal, for within a quarter of an hour my father's hounds will be nosing you out. And when they catch you, I can promise you that Robert de Villacours de la Franché will show little mercy to a common soldier who has insulted his only son!'

The man stared down at Geoffrey, his brown eyes narrow. He shook the whip-lash free from the lad's arm. Then he coiled it slowly and hung it over his saddle-bow. His movements were so studied, so deliberate, that even the angry young nobleman was impressed. This man's hands did not shake, nor did his voice tremble as he turned to the girl, and, bowing slightly from the saddle, said gently, 'I beg you, lead me to Robert de Villacours de la Franché, if that is your father, lady. I shall have something to say to him about his son, something which will make that son forget his high-flown talk of hounds and mercy to common soldiers. Pray, lead on, lady, and I will follow.'

Then, without another glance at Geoffrey, the man turned his horse and rode after Alys, who by this time had gathered her wits again and was not displeased to see her quick-tempered young brother dealt with so firmly. 'He has too much of his own way,' she thought, 'since mother died. It is time someone put him in his place....'

Crestfallen by the loss of his hawk, his dagger, and his dignity, Geoffrey mounted his black horse once again and swung round to follow them down the hill.

If he knew anything, his father would deal short shrift to this shabby fellow – who could expect to find himself chained to the dungeon wall before half an hour was past ... and lucky if he escaped a whipping at that!

Geoffrey's spirits rose at the thought. He even began to whistle as he descended the slope, a light little tune that he had picked up from a troubadour of Provence a few days before.

2. The Castle of Beauregard

As he rode on down the grassy slope, Geoffrey's spirits rose still higher, in spite of the loss of his hawk, for the castle of Beauregard below him, almost golden in the sunshine, circled by its blue moat, lay safe and solid and comfortable.

And he thought of his father's words to him, only the night before, as they sat together by the central hearth in the great hall, with the men-at-arms singing and joking together about the long oak tables. 'One day, my son,' said Robert de Villacours, 'this house will be yours, to maintain and to add to, as the mood takes you, just as I have done, and my father and grandfather before me did.'

Geoffrey looked down with pride on Castle Beauregard. True, it was not one of those massive affairs, with many keeps and immensely high walls, and a great clanking portcullis. But then, who needed such castles now! They were as dead as the Great Circle at Carnac, where the Druids used to worship.

He gazed down at Beauregard, running his eye the length of the place – from the octagonal North Tower with its arrow-slits and battlements, along the adjoining great hall, with its four jutting gables and their leaded windows, then on to the Solar, that snug little room where the thick woollen tapestry hid the rough stonework of the walls and kept the draughts out. He remembered his mother and her ladies working at that tapestry, day in, day out, when he was a little lad playing on the floor with a wooden horse that the castle carpenter had made him. That tapestry had once shown a gay hunting scene, in reds and blues and deep yellows; but already it was faded with sun and the rain that beat through the little windows. It was hard to pick out all the figures in the picture. The serving women said that this was because the dyes had not been fast ones! But the Lord of the Manor, Geoffrey's father, only clucked with his tongue, as though dyes and tapestries did not matter very much. ... Geoffrey thought that his mother would have minded, if she had been living still, for she had been proud of the tapestry. He remembered that when it was finished she had turned to one of her Ladies to say, 'There! Now let anyone talk to me of Queen Matilda and that silly piece of stitchery at Bayeux!'

Geoffrey blinked away a tear and then looked across at the squat South Tower, with its conical leaden roof. That was where he and Alys used to hide, scuttering like mice round and round the spiral stairway that lay in the thickness of the wall, whenever they had been so outrageous as to incur their gentle mother's anger.

He recalled the occasion when he and his sister had last taken refuge on the roof. They had done something so terrible that had the drawbridge across the little moat been down, they would have raced over the cobbled courtyard, past the Gatehouse, and have hidden in the Church which lay outside the Castle bounds.

It had been the day before one of the festivals, Geoffrey forgot which, there were so many; but he recalled that the cooks had been working like demons, inventing stuffings, cracking bones for the tender marrow, plucking wild-fowl, and polishing the pewter and wooden dishes.

He and Alys had wandered down into the cellar below the Solar, and there, in the cool dusk, had sampled some of the barley beer from the great hogshead kept for the fifty men-at-arms. It had been grand fun, each turning the spigot while the other caught the liquid in cupped hands.

But, unfortunately, they had forgotten to pull the wooden tap over hard when they had quenched their thirst, and it had not been long before they had heard the serving men calling out in horror as they splashed ankle deep in the precious beer.

And this time they were not left long in peace on the roof of the South Tower. This time their crime was beyond the forgiveness of the parched men-at-arms just off duty at the dusty Gateway. Usually the soldiers pretended not to know where the children were hiding, when the Chatelaine sent for them to punish them; but this time there was no such pretence!

As they crouched on the leaden roof, wishing they were as small as spiders, a head appeared at the top of the spiral stairway. A head with bushy red moustaches and eyebrows, with pale blue eyes that gazed at them in silent reproach for a while before becoming angry. It was the Captain of Arms, Jehan himself, who had come to fetch them.

He did not say a word, but merely saluted them, as was their right, being the children of the Lord of the Manor. Then he took Alys by one plait and Geoffrey by one ear, and marched them down to the Solar, where their mother sat waiting for them, her arms folded.

That was serious, they could tell, because usually she was weaving, or spinning, or stitching, and always singing some little roundel or catch, about knights or love, that she had picked up from the wandering music-men, the troubadours.

But now she was silent and her lips were tight together. She gazed at her two children sadly and shook her head.

At last she said, 'Did you cause all that beer to be wasted?'

Alys began to snivel, but Geoffrey stepped as far forward as the soldier's grasp would let him and said, 'Yes, mother, it was our fault, we did it.'

His mother merely sighed and nodded. 'At least you are honest,' she said as she rose and went to the door, 'I have that to be thankful for.' Geoffrey's heart rose.

Then she stopped and without looking back said gently, 'Beat both of them, Jehan. And as you do so, remember that your men will go short of beer tomorrow – so do not be too merciful.'

When she had gone, Jehan laid them both over the table in turn and smacked them soundly with the stiff leather scabbard of his sword. Geoffrey would have died rather than cry out, although Jehan laid on quite soundly. But when he came to Alys his strength seemed to have flagged somewhat. She was actually smiling when he stood back and saluted them both once more.

Then they were put in the little triangular closet, just off the Solar, to calm down, and the thick oaken door was bolted on the other side. Here there was a small slab of stone set in one corner as a seat, but Geoffrey did not feel like sitting down. Instead, he let his sister sit while he stood on tiptoe and gazed through the narrow window with its thick grey glass that made the countryside outside look so distorted.

'I'd run away to the Holy Land and be a crusader if I could,' he remembered saying in his anger.

But Alys had only smiled and said, 'After all, brother, we deserved it. Think of those poor thirsty soldiers tomorrow! Besides, there aren't any Crusades now! Isn't the Pope always saying something about that? Hasn't he called us all cowards, or something, for giving up so easily to the Infidel? No, you can't be a crusader if there are no Crusades, simpleton!'

As Geoffrey cantered over the last stretch of meadowland before reaching the Gatehouse, he thought of these things and was sad. But then his spirits rose as he saw the man on the horse before him turn round and smile back, as though he and Alys were sharing a joke about Geoffrey.

'Ha!' the boy said to himself, 'but wait until my father hears what I have to say! You'll smile on the other side of your swarthy face then, I warrant you!'

Geoffrey gave his horse a sharp kick, urging the spirited beast onwards towards the drawbridge. But the others reached it twenty paces before he did. Alys signed to the guard and the bridge came down with a clatter on its chains. They rode across and into the courtyard. When Geoffrey arrived at the Gatehouse, cross at being so out-distanced, the guard was still gazing after the blackhaired stranger who had entered the castle.

Geoffrey reined in his horse and stared down at the man.

'Well,' he said, as sternly as he could manage, 'and have you no salute for your master's son, soldier?'

The man came out of his dream and tried to smile. He stamped his armoured feet on the ground and clumped his heavy pike-butt down before him.

'I'm sorry, young master,' he said, 'but I was so taken aback, to see who had arrived with the young mistress!'

'What!' almost shouted Geoffrey, 'that blackhaired rogue! What is there about him to surprise anyone, heh?'

The guard came near to letting fall his pike and his eyes were round with wonder. He even stammered. 'But, master,' he said, 'do you not know who that knight is? I thought all France knew him.'

Geoffrey's eyes blazed, 'Well, for your information, soldier,' he said, 'allow me to tell you that there is one nobleman in France who does not.'

Then he rode forward to find his father.

3. Bertrand de Gisors

GEOFFREY pushed his horse on, across the crowded courtyard, among the many men who worked there, blacksmiths, farriers, fletchers – even the cooks, chopping away busily at the carcase of an ox in readiness for the evening meal. Most things were done in the courtyard; here the men-at-arms practised sword strokes with each other, using heavy staves instead of weapons; here fresh young horses were put through their paces; and here, after a week's hunting, sleeping out under hedges and in ditches, Geoffrey and his father, and any other gentlemen who might be staying at Beauregard, bathed.

On such occasions, the courtyard was cleared, and a great barrel was rolled out into the yard, in the lee of the wall so as to be clear of draughts. Then the serving men and women would run out with skillets and buckets of hot water, until the cask was filled chest-high. So, amid much laughter and splashing and general horse-play, the begrimed huntsmen would scrub themselves and each other, using coarse sand or pumice to remove most of the dirt.

It was while they were so engaged that the young priest, Gerard, who lived at Beauregard, had drawn them all, to put them, suitably tinted in browns and pinks and blues, in a Book of Hours which he was making, in the off moments when he was not struggling to teach Alys and Geoffrey how to write and to read Latin, or when he was not assisting the parish priest at the little church of St Paul, which lay just outside the castle bounds, beyond the moat.

But these things were not on Geoffrey's mind as he handed over his horse to a stableboy, who ran to take his reins. He was now wondering who the blackhaired stranger was and what he could tell his father about the lost hawk.

The second of his problems was soon solved. The head-

22

falconer, old Gil, who boasted of having served the King of England himself as an austringer in his early days, shuffled up to him, half-relieved, half-angry, tugging at his rusty forelock almost in defiance.

'Fine how-do-ye-do this is, my lordling, I must say!' he said. 'Here's you just arrived – and the tiercel here, screaming to be hooded, a quarter of an hour before you! What sort of falconry is that, may I ask, master?'

Geoffrey gazed at him in astonishment. 'What!' he said. 'Has my hawk come back to the mews alone?'

The falconer nodded. 'Aye,' he said, 'and screeched like a demon at the lad who tried to lure her. She's safe enough now, my lord, but there's something strange going on. Someone has upset her, I'll be bound!'

Geoffrey nodded, glad not to have lost his hawk, glad not to have his father to settle with. He patted the old man's shoulder and smiled. 'I'll give a silver piece to the lad who lured her down,' he said, and hurried away towards the steps that led up to the Solar, where his father would be.

Robert de Villacours, his grey hair cropped short to avoid tangles during the hunting season, dressed in his long black velvet gown that was threadbare at the elbows and ragged at the hem, where he trod on it going up the many stairs of Beauregard, was standing with his arms round the black-haired stranger. Geoffrey almost ran up the stone steps, bewildered and still furious with the man who had so damaged his pride before his sister.

Robert de Villacours turned and smiled at his son. 'Kneel, boy,' he said gently, 'before Bertrand de Gisors, a Knight of the Temple, who is back from the Holy War after half a lifetime of fighting against the Infidel.'

Geoffrey gazed in awe at that smiling, straight face, at the white teeth and the twinkling gold ear-rings. He had heard, times without number, of Bertrand de Gisors – his father's oldest friend, and one of the greatest swordsmen France had ever borne.

He knelt before the squat, blackhaired man, his own

head bowed in obedience to his father's command. After all, he thought, it was no dishonour to be bested by such a warrior ... but who would have thought that a man like this would ride the countryside like some outworn kempery-man, on a horse fit only for the knacker's yard!

Then he heard Bertrand de Gisors speak, and his voice was low but strong. 'You have a fine son here, Robert,' he said. 'A rare young gamecock. If God had given me such a boy, I'd count myself the luckiest man in France.'

Then Bertrand touched him on the shoulder, meaning him to rise. Geoffrey did so, half-frowning, half-smiling. Bertrand de Gisors took his two hands in his own, and in a voice hardly more than a whisper said, 'There is an ancient Arabic proverb which says, "Only the fool weeps over yesterday". Let us be friends, Geoffrey. I am your servant.'

Geoffrey half bowed before this man, then turned to see Alys smiling at him, her eyes lit with mischief. 'I am your servant, Sir,' he mumbled.

Then his father clapped him on the shoulder. 'Well said, lad,' he laughed. 'Now off with you to the priest. It's Latin that makes a good warrior, eh, Bertrand?'

But Bertrand did not answer. Geoffrey's last picture of him was as a squat man, as broad as a giant, almost as short as a boy, whose grin meant neither one thing nor another, but was simply a sign of his great good nature.

4. *Stephen of Cloyes*

BUT Brother Gerard did not want to be bothered that day. He had come to a page of his Book of Hours that needed all his time and patience. They found him embellishing an immense capital letter with gold leaf, burnishing the raised design with a delicate spatula of ivory, and clucking with annoyance whenever his long sleeve came unpinned and swept across his handiwork.

'Go away, children!' he said, wiping a gold-tinted hand across his thin flushed face. 'This work must be finished today if it is to dry properly. We will write together in the morning, after Matins. The light will be better then. Go and read to each other under the apple trees; can't you see I'm busy?'

He went back to his work, a streak of gold across his lined forehead. Geoffrey and Alys withdrew from the little room, glad to be free from their lessons that day.

'Come on,' said Geoffrey, 'we will go to the Solar and listen to the glorious adventures of that redoubtable paragon of all Knights, Bertrand de Gisors!'

Alys made a face at her brother. 'You did not mock him with such confidence when he tumbled you from your horse with one flick of his whip, did you, little brother!'

For an instant Geoffrey's expression was grim. Then he smiled again and said, 'I shall not let you goad me into anger against Bertrand de Gisors. He did what any Knight should do, even though only for a mere girl, and one who really deserved punishment at that! And I count it no disgrace to have been bested by such an experienced soldier.'

They were walking along the oak gallery, above the great hall. Below them a little group of men-at-arms sprawled in the straw about the central fire, gossiping, cleaning their swords, and teasing the cooks who were busy at their work for the evening meal. Suddenly Alys stopped and held her finger to her lips. 'Listen,' she said, 'I can hear father and Bertrand. They are talking about us!'

In the wall, above their heads, was a small square peephole which led into the Solar, and through which the Lord of the Manor looked down on the great hall, keeping an eye and an ear on the festivities below. Usually this aperture was closed on the inside by a small oak door, over which the tapestry was drawn to keep out the draughts; but today, by some oversight, it remained open, and though Geoffrey and Alys would never have thought to eavesdrop in the normal run of things, now they found it impossible not to listen to what was being said, if only because their own names were being spoken.

'But why do you say my children are in danger?' they heard their father ask. 'Surely, this affair does not concern them.'

The deep voice of Bertrand de Gisors came to them, in reply. 'I tell you, friend Robert, all the children of France are in danger – not only Alys and Geoffrey. This thing is a disease as deadly as the plague, as cunning as leprosy. It takes no account of noble birth, but infects all who come in contact with it, nobleman or peasant.'

There was silence for a moment, then Robert de Villacours said, 'But you say this fellow, this Stephen, is merely the son of a shepherd from Cloyes, a simple-minded twelve-year-old! What influence can such a clown have over the children of gentle families, children who have been taught their Latin and know a bit about chivalry and so on. They would not be deceived by such a fellow, surely?'

Bertrand's voice was grave. 'A few scraps of Latin and a smattering of horsemanship are no protection against this boy's enthusiasm,' he said. 'Stephen of Cloyes may only be a shepherd lad, but he has the eloquence of a Bishop! He may only be twelve years old, but he has the confidence of a man. And no one who has heard him would call him simple-minded. ... Indeed, there are a score of learned priests who would follow him to the other end of the world if he but nodded in their direction.'

Now Robert's words came hastily, as though they reflected the agitation in his heart. 'And you mean to tell me that this lad, Stephen of Cloyes, actually forced his way into the Court at Saint Denis and spoke to King Philip himself?'

Bertrand laughed strangely, 'Aye, friend,' he said. 'And he did more than that! He gave the King a letter which he said had come from Christ in person, commanding Philip to assist Stephen with all his might to lead a Crusade of children against the Infidel in the Holy Land.'

The two listeners heard their father's gasp of astonishment. 'This is too much!' he said. 'The fellow should be whipped!'

Bertrand answered slowly. 'He is beyond whipping, Robert. That would not cure him. When the King sent him packing, the lad stood on the steps of the Abbey of Saint Denis and announced to all and sundry that he had heard holy voices which had given him the power to perform miracles! By my faith, he swore that he would cause the seas to part, as Moses did, to let all the children walk dry-shod from France to the Holy Land – and even the priests believed him!'

Robert's voice was full of anger now. 'Then so much the worse for the priests!' he said. 'They are bigger fools than I took them for. But I assure you, friend Bertrand, my own children will not be tricked by such tomfoolery. Geoffrey has a good head on his shoulders, and Alys will be ruled by me in such a matter.'

At the mention of their names, the two children started guiltily. 'Come away,' whispered Geoffrey, taking his sister by one of her plaits.

'Wait,' she said, 'this is most interesting.'

'You are a shameless hussy!' said her brother.

But she only smiled back at him, still listening.

And Bertrand de Gisors said, 'Well, I have warned you, friend, and now I go on to warn others like you who have children. Already Stephen has hundreds anxious to follow him, and in a month's time when they are all to meet at Vendôme, there will be thousands! They will sweep over France like the locusts of the East, and like those locusts they will bring destruction. No family will be safe. No parent will be able to call his children his own. I warn you, friend.'

Alys made a wry face up at the little peephole. Then she followed her brother down into the courtyard.

She found him kicking thoughtfully at a bale of straw, and fingering his chin.

'Well, brother,' she said wickedly, 'and are you already following Stephen to Jerusalem?'

Geoffrey did not look at her as he replied. Nor did he seem to notice that she was teasing him.

'I have often envied the men,' he said. 'They come back with such wonderful tales of adventure and often with masses of treasure.'

Alys thought for a while, then she said, 'I wonder what this Stephen is like? He must be a splendid person to cause everyone to follow him, like that!'

Geoffrey grunted. 'A mere shepherd lad,' he said. 'I'm not concerned with him . . . it's his idea of a Crusade that interests me.'

That evening, after he had eaten a light meal and while there was still light to see by, Bertrand de Gisors rode away from Beauregard, a man intent on a mission.

And when this man had disappeared over the hill, Robert de Villacours called his children up to the Solar.

'*Mes enfants*,' he said solemnly, 'I have something serious to tell you.'

They stood by his big gilded chair.

'Yes, my father?' said Alys, pursing her mouth primly so that she would not smile.

For they already knew what it was their father would tell them. All they hoped was that he would not make them take the oath not to follow Stephen.

He did not; it never occurred to him to do so – he credited them with more common sense than most of the children of France.

'What is considered appropriate for some children, by some parents,' he said, 'does not apply to us, does it, my chickens? My pair of pigeons would not dream of running after a ragged rascal like Stephen of Cloyes, I well know.'

He smiled down at them, from his great carved oak chair, in the candle-light. Alys gazed back at him, her eyes full of mischief.

'Which are we, father,' she said, 'chickens or pigeons? One cannot be both at the same time, you understand!'

Robert de Villacours pretended to snort and to become very cross with her, but she skipped out of his way, and on down the narrow stairs.

5. Strange Meeting and Bad News

SPRING turned to early summer and the tender green shoots of wheat in the manorial fields began to ripen, the lambs to grow too big to feed from their mothers any longer, the young hawks or eyases to become fierce and querulous whenever a hand came too close. And in the vine-growing districts the grapes filled out, giving promise of a good vintage year. It was as though France rustled with newness, with the strange restlessness of growth.

Both Alys and Geoffrey shared this unrest. Often, as the nights lengthened and the amber sunlight struck down across her tambour-frame at a time when she ought to have been thinking of bed, Alys would neglect her embroidery and seek her brother's company. And Geoffrey would be only too ready to leave his writing book, or the piece of armour he was burnishing, to walk with his sister along the river bank, among the sallows and osiers. For they had a secret to share.

Each day brought fresh news of the shepherd boy, Stephen, and his great host of 'Crusaders'. One rider said that almost 30,000 children were making their way from Vendôme, through Tours, and were heading towards Lyons. Another messenger galloped in with the news that children were flocking to Stephen's side from every sort of home, and in defiance of anything their parents might do or threaten.

One evening, as they sat under a wild rosebush near the shallow river, Alys suddenly said to Geoffrey, 'Our castle lies on the easiest route between Tours and Lyons, brother.' Then she stopped, as though uncertain how to proceed.

Geoffrey looked away from her and flung a pebble into the water, slowly and deliberately. 'That is understood, sister,' he said. Then he paused for a moment before finishing. 'I have thought of little else since Bertrand de Gisors spoke of it all. I have dreamed about it almost every night.'

Alys stood then, suddenly alarmed by the hoarse note in her brother's voice. She took a pace towards him and was about to place her hand on his arm to console him, when a sound behind her caused the girl to stop and turn her head.

A man was standing beside the wild rosebush, watching them, his thin dark face twisted in a strangely mocking smile, his black eyes glimmering, half-closed, beneath bushy brows.

Had the girl seen only this face with its deep lines and its twisted expression, she would have taken to her heels without delay, assuming that no one but a lordless man, an outlaw, could possess such a mask of evil. But, as the man came forward from behind the rosebush, Alys saw that he was dressed in a livery which both proclaimed him as harmless, and at the same time provided him with an excuse for travelling the countryside unhampered by the tools of his calling.

For the stranger was dressed in a long ragged gown of parti-coloured fustian, red on one side, yellow on the other; his sleeves hanging almost to the ground. About his thin waist he wore a narrow belt of blue leather, into which was thrust a silver-mounted flute of ebony. On his head danced a red cap in the shape of a cock's comb, from the sides of which hung two asses ears, on the points of which dangled little bronze bells, which jingled with every movement he made.

With the shock of meeting, Geoffrey's hand slid almost by habit to the hilt of his dagger, for it was his duty to protect his sister; but the stranger held up his hands, palm forward, as though to signify his peaceful intention. Then he fell on his knees before Alys. '*Mademoiselle*, I serve you,' he said. Turning, he bowed his head before Geoffrey. '*Seigneur*,' he said, 'I honour you.'

For a moment Geoffrey stared down at him, with all the arrogance of a young nobleman confronting a serf.

Then he said, 'It would be wiser of you in the future to announce your presence from a distance, fellow, before breaking in on the privacy of gentlefolk like this. It would be safer, too.'

The man bowed his head humbly once more, though Alys thought she saw that mocking smile creep over his features again as he did so.

In a low voice he said, 'You are as wise as you are merciful, *mon Seigneur*. One day the fair land of France will resound with your fame; of that I am certain.'

Geoffrey preened himself at the man's words. He was not accustomed to such flattery, for his father had always treated him with straightforward, honest common sense. Robert de Villacours believed that the world was a hard place to be in and wanted his only son to be prepared for the trials and tribulations that life must inevitably thrust on him one day when he came to inherit Beauregard and its lands . . .

So the stranger's flattering words had their effect on the boy, and he suddenly felt very grown up and generous. He sat down on the grass, with something of a lordly air and keeping his distance from the stranger so as to indicate the difference in their stations. 'You are something of a musician,' he said, pointing to the flute in the man's belt. 'So I presume that you are walking from castle to castle to earn your bread?'

The man nodded, causing the bells on his cap to jangle once again. 'Aye, master,' he said, 'I have the touch of the thing and have played for my meat and drink from Antioch to Paris and back again.' He drew the flute from his belt and held it in his hand for a moment so that they should see it clearly in the early summer sunshine.

It was a beautiful instrument, carved intricately from bell to mouthpiece with little figures of men and women dancing, of animals prancing, and of vine-clusters and flowers. Even the broad silver bands at each end of the flute were delicately chased with flowing decorations.

Alys could not help herself. 'But, that is magnificent, stranger!' she said. 'I have not seen such another in my life!'

The man's eyelids lowered. 'Your taste is as flawless as your beauty, my lady,' he said with a smile, seeming not to notice that Geoffrey gave a sudden snort. 'This instrument was made, countless years ago, by some old craftsman of Arabia. As you will see, the inscriptions on these silver bands are in the ancient language of that country.'

He held the flute towards Alys, but did not allow her to touch it. 'What do the inscriptions mean?' asked Geoffrey, abruptly.

The man shook his head. 'Who knows?' he said. 'Ah, who knows! Someone once told me that they are old spells, the old magic of Arabia; but I am not learned in such things. I am a simple fellow, young lord, a mere juggler and musician. I leave learning to the great ones, the important folk – such as you are.'

Geoffrey did not like the twist of the man's lips as he spoke those words. He put on what Alys always called his 'grand seigneur' look.

'Very well, fellow,' he said sharply, 'then play the thing! Do not sit looking at it all day, like a country wench before a sweetmeat booth at a Fair!'

Once more the stranger bowed. Then he set the flute to his thin lips and blew down it softly, his slim fingers moving up and down on the holes as nimbly as a company of dancers.

At first it seemed to Alys that the music was weird and uncouth, but then she suddenly thought that it was the most beautiful sound she had ever heard. The sweet full notes seemed to weave in and out of each other like a coloured tapestry, and in those sounds the girl heard the story of creation, of the richness and complexity of Nature. Yet, to Geoffrey the music meant something else; it was glory in battle, with the scarlet banners waving in the wind, and the jingle of harness and armour, and the thundering of hooves at the charge....

And when the last note had fallen to its close and the sounds of the river and the evening breeze in the trees had returned again, the boy said breathlessly, 'Stranger, there is magic in that flute. Such music might lead an army half-way across the world.'

But the man merely bowed his head humbly as he wiped the flute and tucked it into his belt once more.

'I am honoured that you should think so, lord,' he said quietly.

On their way back to Beauregard, Alys was still in a trance of rapture. It was as though she did not dare speak, for fear of breaking the dream which the music had conjured up for her.

At the drawbridge, the guard stared in amazement to see the tall stranger striding between the children, the long skirt of his coloured habit swinging. But he recollected himself in time to give the required salute, and so the three passed across the courtyard on their way to the great hall.

Yet even as they mounted the first steps, a shadow fell across their path. The young priest, Gerard, stood looking down at them strangely, a frown wrinkling his pale forehead. And when the laughing, dark-faced stranger stared up at him, the priest made the sign of the cross hurriedly and put on a stern expression.

'My lord and lady,' he said quickly, 'your father has sent me to find you. He commands you to go to him without delay. There is something he wishes to say to you, privately.'

He looked down, pointedly, at the stranger, who smiled back at him and, shrugging his shoulders, sat down on the stone steps.

'I pray you, lord and lady, have no thought for me,' he said. 'I can amuse myself. I am well received if I have a stone step to sit on.'

Then he pulled the flute from his belt once more and with a sly smile began to sound a phrase or two.

The priest took Alys by the hand and drew her up the inner stairway towards the Solar. Geoffrey followed them, frowning, the sound of the flute already tugging at his legs.

In the shadowy room, Robert de Villacours paced up and down, a glass of Malvoisie from the green flask on the oak table in his hand. He had the appearance of a man who was bracing himself to carry out a task for which he had little taste.

'My dear ones,' he said, after Geoffrey and Alys had knelt before him, as was required of dutiful French children, 'I have news for you; news which, perhaps, you will not welcome at this moment, but news which, nevertheless, I am bound in honour to tell you.'

Then he paused so long, trying to find the right words for his message, that Alys said impatiently, 'I implore you, father, to put us out of our misery. What have you to tell us?'

Robert de Villacours stood above his daughter, his hand on her shoulder, as though to give himself the courage to speak.

'My children,' he said quickly, 'your dear mother has been dead two years now. We have felt her loss deeply, the three of us, that is understood. But we must also understand that children of your age need a mother, and a castle like Beauregard needs its mistress, its châtelaine.'

He paused for a moment, at a loss. Geoffrey's face clouded. 'So you are going to marry again? Is that it, father?'

Robert de Villacours nodded gently.

'This evening a messenger has come from the widowed Angeline de Guicher, accepting my offer of marriage. I am overjoyed and hope that my children will share that joy! She is a good woman.'

Alys gave a great sob and pulled away from her father's hand. Then, with a flurry of skirts, she turned and ran out of the room. Geoffrey looked up into his father's face. 'She may be a good woman, as you say, father,' he heard himself saying, 'but she can never take the place of our mother.'

Greatly daring in his sadness, the boy turned away and strode to the door. He halted for a second when his father called out his name, but then went on, past the priest Gerard, who stood in the dusky passageway, and so down the stairs.

Alys was sitting on the bottom step, weeping, her face in her hands. Geoffrey stood over her, biting his lips to keep back his own tears.

At last he touched her gently on the shoulder and said, 'Do not cry, my sister. What will be, will be; and this perhaps makes our path easier to tread!'

From the great hall came the sound of the merry flute. The children went towards the doorway, where the torches were already flaring and spluttering in the evening breeze.

6. *The Magic Flute*

SMOKE hung in the high rafters, like a canopy of thick grey gauze, which eddied backwards and forwards as the evening breezes worried at it from the windows of the great hall.

Below, about the long tables, the men-at-arms lounged at their benches or leaned against the wall, listening to the flute-player, their beef and ale forgotten for the while in the magic of the world which the glittering music unfolded for them.

And, as he played, his head swaying from side to side in time to his melodies, the musician watched them all intently, his dark eyes swinging from one to the other, judging the effects his tunes were having upon these simple-minded soldiers.

When his last cadence had fallen to stillness, the men at the tables seemed to wake from a deep sleep; a rustle passed down the hall; a serving-woman gave a sudden start and let fall the pewter ladle she had been holding. The wandering music-maker stared the length of the hall towards her, smiling at her embarrassment.

Then blunt Gil, the Captain of the Guard, rose from his place at the head of the table nearest the fire, his square-cut beard jutting forth defiantly.

'By Saint Michel and all the relics,' he said, 'but we have not heard such music in our lives before. We are indebted to you, minstrel!'

He held out his cup of beer towards the flute-player as though toasting him, then drank off the liquid at a gulp. Then, as the musician watched them all, smiling and bowing from time to time, Gil flung a silver coin into a wooden dish and passed it down the table. Each soldier added a piece to the store, anxious to reward the man in the parti-coloured gown. A serving-wench ran forward and, scooping the money into her apron, went with it to the wanderer.

For a moment he looked at her as she stood smiling before him. Then he said, 'I can only take this gift from one who can sing as well as I can play. So sing, fair one, sing!'

Then all the men began to laugh, for it was well known that Magdalen, for all her pretty looks and golden hair, had a voice like a rusty key struggling to turn in a lock. The girl flushed and lowered her eyes.

'You mock me, traveller,' she said. 'I have never been able to sing a note.'

The man placed his hands upon her shoulders and said, 'Then it is time you began now! You shall sing the ballad of Young Maurice and his love for Alison.'

Tears stood in the girl's eyes now at the laughter which rose behind her. 'But I do not know the words,' almost sobbed the girl.

Alys, standing by the door with her brother, whispered, 'Oh, how cruel to mock poor Magdalen like that! I will make him stop it!' But her brother's hand restrained her. 'Wait,' he said. 'Things are not what they seem, sister.'

And, true enough, after a flourish of notes on the flute, the girl turned to face the soldiers in the hall, her face now smiling, her voice ringing forth, clear and melodious as a bell.

> 'Young Maurice rode a milk-white steed,
> His sword-hilt was of gold;
> And all the ladies of fair France,
> Yearned for this knight so bold.'

The song told how Maurice mistook the tawny-haired Alison for a red deer in the forest one day, and shot her with an arrow. It was a sad story and ended softly in a minor key.

When Magdalen's voice had faded and the flute was heard no more, a great hush came upon the hall, for all the men there knew that this kitchen wench had never sung before. As for Magdalen, she let slide the silver coins into the minstrel's open pouch and then walked back between the tables, radiant and wide-eyed, like a girl in a shining dream.

For a little while, the flute-player bent down behind a solid backed wooden chair, so that his body could not be seen.

But his hands galloped towards each other along the top of the chair in imitation of two knights at a tournament. The illusion was so complete the men-at-arms gasped. Gil called out, 'Do not let them fight *à l'outrance*, my friend, or you'll lack a hand to play your flute with!'

At this, Geoffrey let out a sudden guffaw – and then saw the flute-player rise slowly from behind the chair and smile towards him, mockingly.

'Come forth, my young lord,' he called down the hall. 'Come forth and bring your noble sister. We will think of another ballad of the sad ancient times that will do credit to your noble voices.'

The men-at-arms turned and gazed at the children, shocked that the wandering minstrel should dare to tease them so, yet interested to see how they would answer the man. Alys shrank back before the minstrel's dark-eyed stare, but Geoffrey took a pace forward, his jaw set, as though he might be about to put this fellow in his place, his hand upon the pommel of his dagger.

But even as he moved, his face seemed to lose its resolution; and his hand fell limply to his side, as though he had come under the power of a spell which was beyond his strength of mind to break. 'Master ...' he whispered. 'Master ...'

Then, as all eyes were turned upon the boy and men began to nudge each other in wonder, another figure appeared in the doorway, a dark-robed figure whose one hand went protectingly about the shrinking Alys, whose other hand pointed, accusingly, at the still-smiling minstrel.

'Stop!' called out the clear voice of Brother Gerard. 'Cease this godless magic, you in the garments of a jester! Have done with this wanton mockery and go your ways!'

Never before had the soldiers seen this gentle priest so moved by anger. His eyes blazed and his head was thrown back like that of a general commanding his pikemen or archers.

Even rough-voiced Gil, the Captain, was impressed. 'Yon priest has the makings of a soldier, by Saint Michel and all the relics!' he muttered. 'I'd give him a place in the guard any day he asked me for a sword!'

What might have happened then, no man knows.

For, as the bewildered Geoffrey stood aside, the two men, priest and magician, moved towards each other, one frowning and one smiling, their wills locked in combat like the antlers of two furious stags.

But even as they came within a spear's length of each other, the door of the great hall was flung open with a crash, and the guard from the watch-tower stumbled inside, looking round, wide-eyed, for his Captain.

'Sir,' he called, his voice hoarse with anxiety, 'they are coming down the road towards the castle. The children, Sir! A great army of them, all singing.'

The Captain of the Guard rose to his feet. The bench clattered over behind him. 'The children?' he said. 'How many are there, man?'

The man shook his head in wonder. 'Thousands of them, sir,' he said. 'More than I have ever seen together in my life before!'

7. The Boy Prophet

THAT night it seemed that the children of half France settled like a vast swarm of locusts about the castle of Beauregard. Alys and Geoffrey, with Brother Gerard, stood on the high South Tower watching excitedly.

At first, from afar off, they heard an immense rustling noise, that seemed to fill the air, like a great wind blowing across a huge field of barley. Then, as the host drew slowly nearer, its torchlights glimmering here and there like distant fireflies, this vague and general rustling broke up into particular and distinguishable sounds – the shuffling of feet, the blowing of horns, the clopping of hooves, the rumbling of wagon-wheels, all intermingled with talking, laughter, shouting, and weeping; the thousand noises of a multitude on the march.

'By all the Saints,' said Brother Gerard, 'but one might imagine that the children of Israel themselves were gathering to cross the Red Sea!'

As the great army came nearer, group after group drew away from the main body to settle here or there, for the night, in the fields, beside the river, alongside the sheltering castle walls, behind the church, and soon each group had a fire blazing and rough tents or shelters erected, so that the countryside far and wide about Beauregard appeared to be in possession of a besieging force, or of a migrating host of nomads.

Then Alys and Geoffrey heard the guards at the drawbridge calling back to their father, 'My lord, he has come, the boy Stephen has come, and commands us to lower the bridge. What are we to do, master?'

And the voice of Robert de Villacours rang out clearly through the dusk, 'I have never refused hospitality to an honest man in my life. If this Stephen means well, let him come into the courtyard and up to fifty of his followers, but no more.'

Then the drawbridge clattered down with a screaming of chains, and a high-sided wagon with solid wheels and drawn by two slavering oxen rumbled across the moat, followed by a great press of children. On either side of the vehicle rode youths, who from the quality of their clothing and their horses were the sons of noble families.

Seated on a straw-filled sack in the fore part of the wagon was a lad of about twelve years of age. From the looks which the others gave him, the obeisances they made before him, Alys and Geoffrey decided that this must be Stephen, the boy prophet who had dared to approach King Philip himself at Saint Denis, and they gazed down with interest at such a person.

Although small for his age and dressed in a drab fustian gown, caught in at the waist by a length of rope, there was indeed something about the lad which held the attention of all who saw him. True, he was not handsome; his almost colourless hair was cropped short at back and sides, and stood out on his crown like a bunch of bleached straw; his eyes were pale and red rimmed; his wrists were thick and raw-looking; his fingernails bitten down to the quick; and when his loose lips parted, it could be seen that many of his upper teeth were missing.

Yet, there was something in the grand movement of his arms, in the impassioned working of his thin throat, something in the crude wooden crucifix which hung by a leather thong from his neck, which gave beholders an impression of strength, of inner force, even of spiritual power.

Suddenly, as the wagon rolled into the circle of light flung out by the clustered torches within the gateway, the boy Stephen rose to his feet. A great silence of respect fell like a heavy cloak over his chattering followers. Even the horses seemed to cease their whinneying and to stand still in the courtyard, letting the evening breezes tease their manes in the dusk.

When Stephen spoke, his voice was rough and hoarse, his speech broad in its dialect and lisping, because of the missing teeth, yet his was the voice of a man rather than of a boy, strong and full of persuasion. He spoke like some rustic Bishop, rather than the undersized son of a serf.

'Lord of Beauregard,' he said, raising his right hand towards the surprised Robert de Villacours, who stood in his black velvet gown on the steps above the courtyard, 'I bless your house and all who follow the teachings of Christ within it.'

A wry smile played over the sombre face of Robert de Villacours. He bowed his fine head slightly and the gold chain about his neck jingled. 'I thank you, Stephen of Cloyes,' he said gravely, 'and now I shall take the liberty of asking you and your immediate retinue to enter my feast hall and to join me in a little supper before you go on your way.'

Alys and her brother were amazed by the tone which had crept into their father's voice. They knew it well enough; it was a tone of kindness, but overlaid with gentle mockery.

But in the dusk they heard Brother Gerard's gasp.

'He should not harbour this young mountebank!' the priest whispered. 'Stephen of Cloyes is abroad on the devil's work, not on that of God!'

It was almost as though the boy in the courtyard had heard the priest's words, for he answered Robert de Villacours in a firm voice, 'I come to do God's work, Robert; and all who follow me come to do likewise. It will ill become me to accept favours for myself and my twelve disciples, while the others go hungry. Let your servants move among my many little ones, who are hungry and crying this night, with bread and meat and warming draughts of wine. I will accept such an offering, Robert de Villacours, but nothing less.'

Then the courtly self-possession of Robert de Villacours seemed to desert him for the moment.

'It is not the custom,' he said sharply, 'for a wanderer to

dictate the laws of hospitality. He must be thankful for what he is given, my friend!'

Through the dusk Stephen's firm voice cut like a keen knife, unabashed and strong.

'I am not bound by the worn-out customs of mankind,' he said, 'I make my own customs as God advises me!'

Then suddenly, as Robert de Villacours gasped with astonishment, Brother Gerard made a pace towards the parapet of the Tower. Alys and Geoffrey had never seen him so angry before. His thin scholarly face seemed to writhe with passion and his pale hands clutched the stones of the low wall as though they would crush them to rubble.

'Be silent, you blasphemous dog!' he shouted, his voice suddenly fierce. 'Who are you to speak for God? Be off with you, back to the kennel you were born in! And thank your stars that you go with a whole hide!'

Down in the courtyard then something happened which caused Alys to shrink with horror. The boy Stephen half-turned and, as he did so, slipped his loose robe from his thin shoulders, so that his back was exposed in the flickering torchlight.

The livid scars of the lash were revealed, for all to see; and after a little while the boy turned, to look up, almost in triumph, towards the parapet of the Tower.

And now he spoke with all the force of a prophet. 'I have already met with other men of a similar turn of mind to your own, priest. They have left their marks upon my back – but not upon my Spirit!'

For a moment Brother Gerard stood speechless, as though ashamed at his own outburst. Then he seemed to recollect himself, and said in a low and even voice, 'I am grieved that a lad such as you are should have met with such treatment; yet that in itself should serve to warn you that you play a dangerous game, Stephen of Cloyes.'

The lad in the cart sat down on the straw-stuffed sack, as though he had become weary suddenly. When he spoke, his voice was that of a martyr.

'The Christ himself played such a game, priest,' he said. 'And, as you will remember, he too was whipped with lashes.'

Now Brother Gerard forgot all his pious resolutions and begun once more to clench the harsh stones of the parapet, his eyes starting, his slender body rocking with anger at this new blasphemy. What he would have done or said, no man knows, for at the very climax of his fury another player moved on to the stage and took charge of the drama.

At first, all that was seen was a smiling dark shadow in the glow cast by the torches. Then there came a high piercing note of the flute, shooting like a swift arrow across the courtyard, to be followed by a cascade of notes which glittered on the ear like sparks from a swordsmith's anvil.

The minstrel stood, smiling up towards the dark turret, his teeth flashing, his ear-rings gleaming, his voice as thin and clear as the winds of winter calling through the blackened boughs.

'Be not afraid, oh little priest!' he called mockingly. 'This honest shepherd lad has not come to steal your place from you!'

Then, as Gerard gasped, the piper bowed low to the dark figure of the Lord of Beauregard.

'Nor be you afraid, Robert de Villacours,' he went on, 'that these poor children shall eat your bread and drink your precious wine. No, they are too proud to do that, Robert de Villacours! Too proud to do anything but serve Christ, and to rid his City of the Infidel! A task which certain knights of valour might be proud to imitate, Robert de Villacours! A task in which I shall count it an honour to lead them!'

Then the man blew a series of strange grace notes on his pipe, so that it seemed as though a host of trumpets had given tongue, bidding all men of good heart to follow into battle.

And so he turned towards the drawbridge, and almost as though spurned on by goads, the oxen and the horses turned with him, and the children on foot followed, as though in a deep dream.

And Stephen of Cloyes passed out of the courtyard of Beauregard, his head still sunk on his breast, towards the flickering camp-fires of his followers, in the broad fields beyond the moat.

And when the last child had gone, Robert de Villacours had to raise the bridge himself, for the guard on duty sat on a stone, his pike at his feet, weeping and remembering his own children, at home in Picardy!

8. *Night Walkers*

OUTSIDE, somewhere beyond the castle wall where the oak tree spinney began, an owl was hooting. Geoffrey sat up in the great curtained bed, listening. It must be almost dawn, he thought, yet he had not been to sleep. His mind was too full of the previous evening's happenings for that.

So that was what the famous Stephen was like! A small ragged fellow with the voice of a prophet and the heart of a lion. A lad who could ride at the head of a multitude towards adventure and glory....

Geoffrey eased himself from the creaking straw mattress and stood by the narrow window, to look out on the moonlight world beyond the castle. Outside, in the fields, fires still glowed here and there, and broad linen banners, bearing the symbol of the Oriflamme, flapped in the first stirrings of the breeze. Soon dawn would slide over the great hill of Saint Antoine, as easily as a falconer's gauntlet over his hand and then this host of children would move on towards adventure. 'A falconer's glove,' thought the boy. 'If I go with them I must leave my hawk, my fierce tiercel that I have trained and gentled so many months.'

He bit his lip in puzzlement. 'Yet, if I stay,' he thought, 'I shall be trapped for ever in Beauregard, perhaps never seeing anything of the world outside France. ... And with that Guicher woman as my step-mother! How can father be so unkind!'

Suddenly he began to put on his clothes, dressing warmly and donning the short jerkin of sheepskin which his mother had made for him, so short a time ago, it seemed. He flung his thoughts away from the jacket or he would have wept outright.

Gritting his teeth, he buckled on his belt, with its shagreen pouch on the left side, its silver-pommelled poniard on the right. Then, carrying his stoutly-shod shoes, he parted the leather curtains behind which Alys slept on the sofa feather mattress and made his way towards the outer door.

And there he paused, to whisper, almost to himself, 'Farewell, sister; sleep well tonight, and may the years which lie before you be happy ones!'

Then he slipped like a ghost through the narrow doorway and on down the worn stone stairs.

And when he had gone, Alys flung back the coverlets of her bed and rose, her hair as close-cropped as that of a boy; and while Geoffrey knelt in the mews, whispering good-bye to his falcon, she rummaged in the oaken coffer where his other clothes lay folded, trying on these nether stocks, this habergeon, that tunic.

And when Geoffrey passed through the little-used priest's gate, at the back of the kitchens, she was less than twenty paces behind him. She watched him let down the narrow plank across the moat, stand for an instant regretting that he could do nothing to raise it behind him, and then she followed him over it, into the meadows.

He did not see her until they had reached the tattered shelter, where Stephen sat, already awake, his disciples around him, the piper by his side smiling.

Stephen looked up at them slowly, his pale eyes red-rimmed with fatigue, and nodded. 'I expected you a little earlier than this,' he said, without emotion. 'You are only just in time, for we shall go on within the hour.'

And after they had knelt before him, placing their hands within his and swearing to follow him loyally, Stephen said, 'I hope you have broken your fast, for we have no food to give you. Yet, all things are achieved by prayer, and maybe God will give you your breakfast at the next village we pass through.'

As dawn broke, the host of children rose from the green fields like a morning mist and went forward quietly, many of them still only half-awake, and all of them hungry.

Alys and Geoffrey were allowed the privilege of walking beside the wagon which carried Stephen and the piper.

At first they were too anxious to get safely away from Beauregard to complain; but when the castle was out of sight and the hard dusty road began to be trying to feet more used to stirrups than to walking, Geoffrey sighed, 'If only we had our horses!'

Alys slapped him on the shoulder, already like a boy, and said, 'Aye, if we had tried to bring our horses, we should not be here now, for they could not have got through the priest's gate and over the little plank. And the guard would have stopped us if we had tried to let down the great bridge!'

An hour later they drank from a little stream where village women were already washing the clothes, and shared half a loaf of black bread which a motherly person in a blue smock flung to them from a cottage door. The piper bowed to her and played a little flourish which made her blush.

They ate no more until late afternoon, when they found a dozen hen's eggs among a pile of straw. But this meal was rudely interrupted by a message which came along the great line of walking children.

'There are men-at-arms behind us, coming to seek the two from Beauregard!'

The piper smiled down from the wagon at Alys.

'Jump up here,' he called. 'We can hide a little one like you under the straw. Your brother must put a sack about his head and walk with the others, farther down the road where the crowd is thickest.'

The two obeyed him without question. Stephen did not halt in his praying to notice what they did. His was another world.

PART TWO

*

9. *Strange Interlude*

DURING the days that followed, Alys and her brother often recalled the tense excitement of that occasion. First Gil, the Captain-at-Arms, and then Dickon, a rough Englishman who had taken service under the Lord of Beauregard, had come storming along the dusty road, kneeing their horses forward among the crowds of children, pushing them aside and threatening to lay a whip lash on any who stood in their way.

Gil passed so close to Geoffrey that the boy could have taken hold of his stirrup-iron if he had wished. But it was Dickon who first reached the lumbering wagon and pulled his great chestnut stallion across the path of the slavering oxen. Alys, under the straw, did not need to be told that the man was near at hand – there was no mistaking his terrible accent!

'Holà, mes braves!' he shouted, holding up his gauntleted hand and bristling his reddish beard. 'Where are the two runaways, the lad and the lass of Beauregard? I know they be somewhere among you here.'

There was a silence while the man reined in his pawing stallion.

'Come now,' he called again, 'you in the wagon there, you with the crucifix! Have ye seen the two runaways?'

Suddenly Stephen of Cloyes seemed to awake from a dream. He stood up in the wagon and pointed a gaunt finger at the soldier.

'Go your ways, red-beard,' he said quietly, 'there are no runaways in this company. Those who are with us have been called by God to fight against the Saracen; they are no runaways.'

For a moment it seemed that Dickon the Englishman would spur his horse up to the wagon and drag Stephen down; but Gil, the Captain, rode forward and signed to the man to withdraw. Then, fixing Stephen with his fierce eye, he said gravely, 'You understand, Stephen, do you not, that the Seigneur of Beauregard has a long arm, and a long whip to go with it?'

The boy stared back fearlessly at the soldier.

'I know that my master, Christ, has a longer arm,' he said. 'And I know that His arm will defend me against the whip of the Seigneur of Beauregard, however long it may be. That is my answer.'

Gil the Captain flushed and bit his lower lip angrily, but there was nothing he could say in answer to the boy's simple words, and it was while he sat there, undecided, that the piper put his flute to his lips and began to play a tune, a tune so gentle, so dainty, that it seemed to come into existence by itself, without the aid of man; but, once in being, it seemed to fill the head, the heart, the understanding. .... In it were the strength of the oak, the fury of the north wind, the sly trickery of the grapes of Bordeaux. It captured the legs no less than the brain, and soon the children who stood about Stephen's wagon began to laugh as the horses on which the men-at-arms were mounted began to prance, to nod their heads, and at last, taking the law into their own control, to turn and amble away, along the road by which they had come only a few minutes before.

Gil and Dickon tugged, helplessly, at the reins and struck with their spurred heels at their horses' flanks. And so, at last, they disappeared among the surging masses of children, masked by the high clouds of dust which rose from the dry highway.

And when they had gone, Alys came from under the heap of straw where she had been hiding and said, 'I give you my thanks, Stephen, for protecting us so.'

But the lad looked away from her as though in disgust.

'May God forgive me for speaking a little less than the truth,' he said. 'And may He make you and your brother worth the price I must pay for you when the last reckoning is told.'

Alys did not understand what he meant, but just then the piper gave her a nudge, and winking merrily at her behind Stephen's back, started up with a jolly marching song that drove away the girl's seriousness and set the feet of all tramping as though in time to a great drum.

And that was always the way it was. Whenever a difficulty arose of any sort, the piper seemed to be there to soothe it away and to smooth everything out with his flute. Through woodland, fresh cornfields, above vineyards, the great army of children went, sometimes laughing, but more often trudging wearily in the heat of the day, with the silver sounds of the flute in their ears.

And though, as June became July, and they drew nearer the City of Lyons, the countryfolk seemed to have less and less to spare for them, always after the piper had thrown the net of his magic over a hamlet, or village, or even a town, kindly women would come out of their houses with gifts of bread, or meat, wooden bowls of broth, or trays of honey-cakes. Not that there was ever enough food to satisfy that avid multitude.

Yet strange things happened on that weary march south. Once, not more than a league from the Rhône, in a little valley where the stream had shrunk so much in the summer that even a child of three could stride across it, the piper blew a queer little tune as a covey of partridge was passing, and four of the birds seemed to collide in mid-air and fell like stones to the ground.

On another occasion the hurrying children came upon a stag, caught by the antlers in a holly thicket. .... And yet again, when many of them whimpered aloud with hunger, the piper played his gayest gigue, and round the next bend of the sunken road they came upon a baker's wagon, on its side, an axle broken. Neither baker nor horse was to be seen and the loaves, some of them still warm, were scattered here and there upon the grass.

Each night, as the children lit their fires, clustering about the glowing twigs as hunched as Tartars, thinking of the cosy homes they had left, consoling themselves with the glory that was to be theirs when they had freed Jerusalem from the Infidel, Stephen would walk among them, stopping here and there, his right hand raised, to call his followers to prayer. Though most of them were of his own age, and some of them considerably older, there were among them many little ones who could hardly understand what Stephen was saying, or even why they were there, listening to him.

It was one of these little children that came near to changing the course of Alys's life.

One night, as she sat at Stephen's feet, in the glow of the campfire, listening to the shepherd lad's impassioned words, Alys noticed a small girl of about five years, sitting opposite her. The child, whose clothes hung in tatters about her thin body, was whimpering with hunger and swayed with exhaustion as she rubbed her dark-rimmed eyes with fragile knuckles.

'Look, Geoffrey,' said Alys. 'The poor little one is suffering. She needs someone to care for her.'

But Geoffrey's attention was caught by the words and gestures of the preacher and he gestured impatiently to silence his sister.

'Be quiet, Alys,' he said. 'Listen to Stephen of Cloyes. There is such magic in his words as may not be heard anywhere else in France.'

Alys was silent then, but Stephen's words gradually lost their meaning for her, and all she knew was a great tenderness for the little child.

Quickly, she rose and, skirting the fire, went to the small girl. Bending over her, she placed a hand on the pale forehead. It was feverishly hot. The little girl lowered her hands and gazed up at Alys with great dark eyes.

'Take me home, *Madame*,' she whimpered, the tears running down her cheeks. 'I want to go back to *Maman* and the chickens.'

Alys was close to tears herself at the words, but putting her arms about the crying child, she picked her up and rocked her gently, trying to soothe her.

Stephen's light eyes seemed to focus on Alys for an instant and, in the midst of his exhortations, he said thickly, 'They who would serve God must be prepared to suffer. Let him

who complains of such suffering return to the unrighteous comforts, the slothful pleasures of his home. There is no place here for those who weep at the task they have undertaken.'

For a moment Alys stood aghast, staring at the boy prophet. Then her anger with him burst forth, before she could control her words.

'Shepherd,' she heard herself saying, amazed at the contempt in her voice, 'the Master whom you profess to follow counselled greater kindness to his little ones than you do, in your arrogant pride. This child is sick, and all because she followed you, poor witless mite! If your heart is so miserable that it can contain no pity for such a one, then I for my part want no more of your Crusade!'

The children clustering round the fire gasped at these words, and one of the noble youths who rode beside the wagon and was now holding up a red banner bearing the symbol of the Oriflamme, stepped forward, his hand raised to strike Alys for her forwardness.

But suddenly there was a scuffling sound from the shadows beyond the fire, as Geoffrey sprang between his sister and the angry youth, his hand already on the pommel of his dagger.

'Stand off, clown!' he shouted. 'Wave your flag against blackamoors, not against young women of good birth! I warrant you, if you come a pace nearer I'll save you the trouble of walking to the Holy Land, that I swear!'

This was too much for the young nobleman. With a cry of fury, he flung down the banner and sprang back a yard as he tugged at the short sword in his belt. Then, teeth bared white in the fireglow, he stood on guard, the blade of his sword pointing at Geoffrey's throat, glinting wickedly in the starlight.

'Come on then, scullion,' he said. 'Make good your boast. No one has ever threatened Jean de Parchet and gone scot free! Come on, I say!'

10. *Sick Child*

THEN everything seemed to happen at once. As Jean de Parchet lunged forward at Geoffrey, Stephen of Cloyes flung himself between the two boys, his arms outstretched, intending to separate them. The children round the fire heard him give a quick gasp, and then Alys found herself crying aloud, 'Look! He is wounded!'

A trickle of blood ran down Stephen's arm. He clutched it, whitefaced, and suddenly knelt to the ground, his tousled head bowed.

Jean de Parchet lowered his sword-point, which trembled, red in the firelight. Then the weapon fell with a thud on to the grass and Jean stared down at the shepherd boy from Cloyes, his eyes wide with fear.

For a while there was a deep silence, broken only by the whimpering of the child who lay in the protective arms of Alys. Geoffrey sheathed his dagger and went forward to raise Stephen to his feet, but the lad waved him away and rose, still grasping his wounded arm, to lean against the wagon.

And when at last he spoke, his voice was terrible to hear, laden as it was with a passion beyond his years. His pale eyes seemed to bore deeply into those of the boy who had wounded him.

'Go, Jean de Parchet,' he said slowly. 'Make your way where you will, for there is no place for you by my side from now on.'

For a moment it seemed that Jean would fall on his knees before Stephen; but then his jaw set, he shrugged his shoulders and turned away towards his horse, stopping only to pick up his sword and wipe it with a handful of grass.

But as he set foot in the stirrup, he paused for a moment and gazed back at the group about the fire.

'Stephen of Cloyes,' he said coldly, 'I have served you well and have got little good of it. I left a comfortable home to ride with you and now I shall return to that home. Nor shall I go alone. There are many here who come from my father's lands. They will be only too glad to see their own folk again. Think of me, Shepherd, when next you need a sword to save you!'

Then, with a toss of the head, Jean de Parchet swung his horse round and rode proudly among the fires towards the high road; and as he went, many children, both boys and girls, rose from their places and followed him as in duty bound. And when their number grew great, he turned in his saddle with a sneer and called, 'You see, Stephen the Shepherd? Your power is perhaps not what you thought. Mayhap the sea will *not* open and let you walk to the Holy Land, after all!'

There was a burst of laughter from the road and then the crowd of children moved into the darkness.

The boy, Stephen, looked about him wildly for an instant, as though he had been splashed with ice-cold water. Then he turned his eyes upwards and said, in a voice which trembled with emotion, 'Oh God, if I have acted wrongfully, then punish me. But if I have acted according to Thy Will, then strike Jean de Parchet down in his pride! Let him lie like a dog on the road!'

Alys heard these cruel words with a shock of horror. Then Stephen's knees gave under him and he fell. It was the piper who picked him up and carried him to the wagon, laying him gently on the straw and bandaging the cut in his arm, glowering as he did so, as though the incident had angered him greatly.

That night Alys nursed the little girl, while Geoffrey went among the others in the encampment, begging what food and drink he could to bring strength back to her.

At dawn, they moved on into the outskirts of Lyons. Stephen seemed almost himself again, but the child, who lay beside Alys in the wagon, was now delirious and crying constantly for her mother.

Alys turned a tear-stained face towards her brother, who now marched beside the wagon, in Jean de Parchet's place. 'Brother,' she said weakly, 'if we do not get help soon for this little one, she will die.'

It was at that moment that the piper leaned over and gazed intently at the child. Then he drew away, as though in disgust, blowing through his nostrils.

'Lay that child by the roadside,' he said grimly, 'if you wish to live yourself. The sickness in her blood is beyond man's aid. She has the plague!'

Alys gazed down at the pale wizened face and then up into the piper's dark eyes. In them she saw only harshness and lack of charity.

She turned to Stephen appealingly, but he stared ahead without seeming to notice her.

'What must I do, master?' she asked at last.

Stephen did not turn towards her when he answered.

'What if one of us should die?' he asked. 'We are many and our task is a great one. It will be as God wishes.'

At this, Alys gave a cry of disappointment and anguish, 'How can you be so cruel!' she exclaimed. 'You, who profess to speak the word of God!'

And as the wagon began to rumble over the first cobble-stones of Lyons, she jumped down sobbing, and ran as fast as her burden would allow her, away from the pale-faced boy who sat on the bale of straw.

So intense was her sorrow that it was not until she stopped for breath that she saw her brother's shadow beside her own on the grey pavement.

'There, there, sister,' he said gently, taking the sleeping child from her arms, 'Stephen of Cloyes has been made deaf and blind by his angelic voices and visions; but you are almost as mad as he is in your hasty anger. Come, we must be reasonable now and seek a doctor for this little one.'

Suddenly Alys stopped again and gazed at her brother with wide eyes.

'Brother,' she said, concerned now for the first time, 'do

you not understand – if this little one has the plague, then we, too, stand in mortal danger of it?'

Geoffrey nodded, almost casually, as he answered. 'I have learned this much from Stephen,' he said, 'that if God wills me to take the plague, I shall take it. There is no more to be said. Let us seek a doctor now.'

11. *Gentle Priest*

AT the end of a street so narrow that the overhanging timbered gables seemed almost to touch each other, leaving only
a strip of intensely blue sky above them, Geoffrey and Alys
came out into an open square, three sides of which were
green with nodding foliage, the fourth being taken up by a
white stone church, built much in the style of Byzantium.

In the middle of the square played a small fountain, its
water springing in jewelled gouts, surrounded by a low ledge
of black marble.

On this ledge sat a young man in a grey habit, his head
shaven, a scroll of parchment spread across his knees. He
looked up and smiled at the children, leaving his forefinger
on the word he had reached in his reading. White doves
fluttered about him in the sunshine.

'Good day, my friends,' he said pleasantly. 'You look tired.
Come and sit beside me in the sunshine. It is restful here.'

Geoffrey took off his black velvet cap and made a small
obeisance before the priest while Alys curtseyed with
reverence.

'There is little time for rest, father,' said the boy. 'This
small child is sick with the plague and we wish to find a
doctor who will tend her. I have money in my pouch to pay
for such treatment, I assure you.'

The young priest smiled a little and put down the scroll
from which he had been reading.

'Sometimes money will not buy back a life that is spent,
young friend,' he said, 'however good the doctor may be.
Then there is nothing left but prayer.'

He walked towards them and looked down at the child
gravely, feeling her pulse, examining her gums, turning
back her eyelids. And at length he smiled again and said,
'Let us sit down in the sunshine by the fountain. God's clean

air and warm sun will do this little maid as much good as any doctor's potions. She has no more plague than I have, glory be to God. Sleep and good food are all she needs. She is exhausted beyond all knowing.'

The young priest gazed calmly at Geoffrey, and then with a slight grimace of amusement at Alys. A dove fluttered down and perched on his shoulder.

'You are wise, lady, to borrow your brother's clothes for your journey,' he said. 'Marching with Stephen of Cloyes on these dusty roads calls for something more practical than skirts and bodices.'

The girl looked back at him in amazement. 'How do you know all this, father?' she asked.

The priest looked away across the square for a while. Then he said quietly, 'Your shoes are almost worn through; you speak with the accent of a place farther north – and Stephen's army of crusaders has been expected here for the last week. There is nothing magic about my guessing.'

After a while they went into the church, the young priest carrying the sleeping child. The gentle air was heavy with the scent of incense; sunlight shone on to the myriad-coloured rose window, casting a riot of red and blue and gold upon the whiteness of the far wall; candles burned steadily upon the decorated altar.

Alys said, 'This church is more splendid than our little one at Beauregard.'

The priest smiled and said, 'That is of no account, daughter. They are both God's houses. He is to be found in your little church as often as in the great cathedral in Rome. And perhaps He is to be found more often in the humble shepherd's hut than in any of them.' Then he went through a side door, carrying the child gently, and leaving the two before the altar.

Geoffrey gazed in wonder at the great golden cup which stood before the candles.

'Look,' he said to his sister, 'it is set with rubies and amethysts, and the base is encircled by ivy leaves of silver!'

Alys answered, 'I have never seen so rich a goblet. Not even King Philip himself can have such a treasure.'

Geoffrey bent forward over the altar rail to examine the precious cup.

'Such a thing should be locked away,' he said, 'lest some wandering man forgot his honesty and stole it.'

A dark shadow fell across the nave of the church and the children turned to see the priest again. Now he was not smiling.

'That is God's cup,' he said. 'He who stole it would have Him to consider. Therein lies its safety, my son.'

Then his gravity left him and he smiled again. 'I have left the little one with a good woman who helps in this house of God,' he said. 'She will care for her and one day, God willing, we will find the child's parents and restore her to them. Now let us kneel together and pray.'

And afterwards the priest said, 'I shall have straw laid within the church, my friends, and tonight you, and as many of your companions as care to, shall have shelter here. I understand that the other churches will also be open to them and many of the houses too. The good folk of Lyons wish Stephen of Cloyes well in his Crusade.'

Geoffrey saw a shadow of doubt flitter across the priest's face as he spoke. 'And do you approve of the Crusade, too, father?' he dared to ask.

For a while the priest was silent, then he said softly. 'Who am I to doubt the truth of Stephen's vision? Pope Innocent has said that you children have put the men of France to shame, and I, who am only the humblest of God's servants, must not gainsay that.'

But, as he turned away, he added, 'Yet if I were the father of a family, I might wonder whether I was failing in my trust if I allowed my children to run into such perils as could await you all, once you leave France.'

As they walked back into the centre of the town, he stood in the little square, beside the sparkling fountain, waving to them. Alys gazed back at him. 'Look, Geoffrey,' she whispered, 'the white doves are fluttering about him. He is so good, I think he must be a saint!'

But her brother only smiled and said, 'Come on, we must hurry or there will be no food to be had in the whole of Lyons. The children will have eaten it all up, like a swarm of locusts!'

They let their ears guide their feet then, towards a place where the air was heavy with the sound of dancing feet, cut through by the high shrill sounds of the piper's merry flute.

And when Alys heard that music again, her face lost its sadness. 'Yes, brother,' she said, 'we must go on with Stephen and the piper. Whatever the priest says, I feel that we are on the way to a great and glorious adventure.'

Her brother smiled at her wickedly. 'You are a changeable one,' he said wrily. 'As for me, I want to see the world and to bring home a fortune, like the other crusaders!'

Then they turned a corner and found themselves among the multitude of noisy children once again.

12. *Golden Chalice*

THAT night as Geoffrey and Alys lay snugly in the straw which was spread between the pews and along the aisles and arcades of the church, surrounded by a hundred other children, they recalled the day they had spent in Lyons; the oxen roasting in the great square and the kind-hearted officers cutting off thick slices for all who asked; the good housewives going among the children, their linen aprons heavy with bread and cakes and meat-pies; the dancing and singing, the blessings from the priests, the hundred and one things that happen when a great crowd assembles – merriment and fighting, jokes, pilfering, quarrels, and reconciliations. ... And always Stephen standing high on the wagon, on the base of a statue, or on the ledge of a fountain, raising his right hand and preaching, preaching, preaching – until his voice was too hoarse to be heard any longer, and he fell with exhaustion to the pavement, to be carried away by the good folk to a soft bed by the fire, in one of the near-by houses that seemed to mount, timbered and many-floored, almost as high as the blue summer sky.

And they remembered the piper, capering about the streets, decked up with ribbons and garlands of flowers, in and out of the crowds, followed by laughing children and merry townsfolk, as though there was a magic in his silvery notes that set all eyes aglow and all heels skipping. ...

'He is a good fellow in his way,' murmured Alys, as she snuggled down in the straw near a brazier. 'His music keeps us going, puts life into us when we flag. ...'

But her brother did not answer; he was already fast asleep and dreaming that Brother Gerard had come to fetch him home to do his Latin lessons. And when Geoffrey would not come, Brother Gerard had said, 'But, my boy, your hawk is pining, she needs you. ...'

And in the morning, when the new sun was streaming once more through the rose window, Geoffrey woke and said, 'Do you think my hawk is pining for me, sister?'

But Alys was too busy combing her hair to pay much attention to his question.

Before they left the church to continue their journey towards Marseilles, the brother and sister knelt before the altar and offered up their prayers. They hoped they might meet the young priest who had been so kind to them, but he did not appear before they left.

Outside, on the broad road south from Lyons, Geoffrey said to Alys, 'From his words to us yesterday, I had thought the priest had trust in mankind. Yet it was not so.'

'What do you mean?' asked his sister.

'Did you not observe,' replied Geoffrey, 'that the golden goblet had been removed from the altar? Apparently the priest thought better of it and had come to the conclusion that we were not to be trusted, after all.'

The two marched on in silence then, each deep in thought.

A league south of Lyons something happened which put all speculations out of their minds. Two blue-liveried horsemen, wearing sword and dagger, came scurrying in a cloud of dust along the road after them, shouting on Stephen to halt his wagon. And when he did so, they foraged among the straw until they had scattered the greater part of it on to the dusty road.

Then, red-faced, they turned to the boy prophet and said angrily, 'Where is the golden chalice that you stole from the church?'

But they saw, from his surprised expression and his wide eyes, that Stephen could not answer their question. They turned to the piper who was playing quietly as he leaned against the wagon.

'Where are the two who carried the sick girl to the church?' they demanded.

Even as Alys and Geoffrey stepped forward, they saw the piper point towards them with his flute.

Geoffrey said angrily, 'I am the heir of the Sieur de Beauregard. I am no church-robber, man.'

The blue-coated rider to whom he spoke flushed and said, with rather more respect, 'I speak on behalf of the church, young sir, not for myself. Where is the cup, I pray you?'

Alys stood before the man and said, 'I swear to you by all the relics, and on the memory of my lady mother, that neither my brother nor I have touched the golden cup. Nor have we any knowledge of its whereabouts. That I swear, as I hope for salvation.'

For a while the two men seemed as though they might leap from their horses and clap irons on the girl and her brother; but the children stared back at them so steadfastly that the leader of the two, tugging at his dark moustaches, swung his horse round angrily, and said to his companion, 'Come, friend, we must carry back their answer and then see what is to be done.'

As they spurred away in a cloud of dust, the second man shouted back, 'Have no fear, my precious pair of pigeons, we are not so easily put off! There will be time to catch you again before you reach the Holy Land!' And, laughing grimly, they began their ride back to Lyons.

Alys turned to Geoffrey now and said, 'So one of our company is a thief, brother? That is a bitter pill to swallow.'

Stephen leaned from the wagon and said, 'Do not be so distressed, little sister. The church is rich and lazy. The church surely owes us something for the work we are doing on her behalf. Whoever has the cup will no doubt use it for the benefit of us all, in our Crusade.'

Then, before they could answer him, the piper struck up a merry tune and the procession moved on down the road.

Alys and Geoffrey were greatly troubled by the whole affair, especially since the young priest had dealt with them so generously, but that afternoon something else happened which even overshadowed this mishap, a thing which was to haunt their dreams for many a night afterwards.

13. *Three Riders*

THE foremost company of children were moving along a sunken lane, the sides of which were thick with yellow-flowering gorse, the floor of which was deeply rutted and heavy with a choking grey dust. Now the sun was swinging away towards the west, throwing the lane into shadow, and the thickly-massed children were silent with fatigue, when suddenly, from above them, came a burst of drunken laughter and mocking shouts, and down from a clump of thick-leaved bushes rode three horsemen, their shaggy horses stumbling and snorting and kicking up the turf with great hooves.

The oxen stopped dead, trembling with the shock of fear at the scent of warhorses, and Stephen stood up in the wagon to halt the children who followed closely in his tracks.

The three riders reined in their chargers, roaring drunkenly with a great show of white teeth and black beards. They were all burnt a dark brown by the sun and wore tattered tabards over rusty mail or soiled habergeons. Their harness was cracked and broken, their scabbards so worn that the hacked blades of their heavy swords were exposed, here and there. Each tabard bore a cross, embroidered in silk so faded that its original red had become an almost indistinguishable pale pink. One of them wore a blood-stained bandage about his head; another's arm hung in a sling. All of them carried heavy canvas sacks before them on the saddle.

In the silence that followed their surprise appearance, Stephen raised his right hand gravely and said, 'I give you greetings, crusaders! We who make our way towards the Holy Land salute you who have fought there on behalf of the True Cross. Greetings and blessings upon you!'

The foremost of the three riders laughed aloud at Stephen's words and, kicking his horse forward, rode until

he stood level with the boy prophet. As he approached, Geoffrey could smell that the man had been drinking heavily, and drew his sister towards the tail of the wagon, out of reach of the horse's great hooves.

'Who, in Hell's name, are you, you snivelling puppet, to give blessings to such as us?' asked the rider, a white froth of foam sprinkling his lips. 'Who are you, boy? Answer me, you half-starved rat!'

Stephen of Cloyes looked back at the rider, his light eyes suddenly wide with the shock of this greeting. Then he lowered his hand and said calmly, 'I am such as you may never be, horseman. For I am of God's army, while you, it seems, are of the devil's, despite the sacred livery you wear.'

Even as Stephen spoke these words, the man gave a deep roar of fury, and sweeping out his sword struck the lad with the flat of the blade beside the temple. Stephen gave a groan and staggered sideways, falling into the dust, under the belly of the nearside ox. The piper leapt down and dragged the boy clear, and even as he did so, Geoffrey, furious at this cowardly attack, snatched a heavy banner of the Oriflamme from a boy who stood near by and sprang forward.

'*Dieu et Beauregard!*' he yelled, in the war-cry of his family, and swinging the banner he struck the horseman with all his force across the sword arm.

The man yelled with pain, his sword falling to the ground. Then, with a drunken cry, he plunged spurs deep into his horse's sides, intending to trample down the lad who had so defied him. But the horse, startled by the sudden prick of spurs, excited by the conflict which he sensed about him, reared without warning, his hooves high in the air.

With a cry of fright, the horseman lost his balance and fell backwards to the ground. The great horse plunged again, his hooves striking down on the tumbled rider.

Then, with a whinny of fear, the warhorse swung about and plunged up the far slope, breaking down bushes and scattering clods of turf as it went.

Geoffrey dropped the banner and knelt beside the fallen

man. He lay quite still, his face growing white beneath his tan. His head lolled strangely sideways now.

One of the remaining riders spoke from where he sat, grimly. 'It is too late now to weep,' he said. 'You have killed the man. Can you not see, his neck is broken! That much you have done for him, with your holy banner!'

Alys was kneeling beside her brother now, holding his shaking hand, 'It was not your fault, brother,' she said. 'This man was the attacker. I would have done the same, if I had had the courage.'

Then, to Geoffrey's astonishment, the two riders set their horses at the far slope, up which the other charger had gone, and though their faces were full of anger, they made no attempt to avenge their fallen comrade.

Geoffrey's eyes swept round as he wondered why these men of war should depart so meekly. The answer was immediately plain to him – the length of the sunken lane, every boy stood on guard, waiting to attack the horsemen should they lift a finger against Geoffrey. Some carried cudgels, some knives, some swords.

Even the piper, smiling wickedly, leaned across the back of one of the oxen, a short bow in his hand, the arrow drawn back to the head.

Then suddenly a great cry arose, 'Geoffrey de Beauregard is our war-leader! Stephen and Geoffrey! Stephen and Geoffrey!'

Stephen smiled wanly down at the lad and said, 'I thank you, friend, for doing what you did. As for this man's death, it was an Act of God. God took him in his drunkenness and in the blasphemy of his act against me! I, the chosen one of the Lord!'

But for Geoffrey there was no rejoicing. He went alone into a wood and prayed, on his knees, for forgiveness, while down below Stephen said a perfunctory prayer over the dead body before the others placed it in a grave they had dug by the roadside.

And that night, Geoffrey found it hard to sleep because of

his blood-guilt, even though all the others seemed to regard him as a hero and spoke to him with respect. At last he wandered far down the river, trying to tire himself under the peaceful stars. But his mind was too over-wrought, even so, to let him sleep. So bemused was he, indeed, that when he returned, he could pay little heed to what his sister waited to tell him. Now her message seemed of small importance because of the awful thing that had happened.

'Brother,' she was saying in a low whisper, 'I have made a discovery ... when I went out to look for you, I stumbled upon the piper. He thought that he was alone, secret, but I saw what he was looking at. ... He has the chalice from the church! I saw him slip it into a small sack. ...'

Wearily, Geoffrey turned away from her and said, 'Oh did he? Then he must have stolen it. That is his guilt, not ours, sister. We cannot set ourselves up as his judge, not after what I have done.'

He said no more about the matter, but lay down on his back, his hands beneath his head, staring up at the stars.

And Alys, waking before the dawn, saw that his eyes were still open, as though the weight of his guilt were too heavy to let him sleep.

She reached across and touched his arm. 'Brother,' she said, 'you do wrong to torment yourself over that man's death. How were you to know that his horse would rear, and that he would be so drunken as not to keep his seat in the saddle? Indeed, how were you to know that the fall would kill him? Many men fall from horses every day, but few of them die.'

Geoffrey sat up in the dawn light and looked down at her, his face serious and pale.

'Sister,' he said, 'I am not so easily consoled; the fact remains that I struck the man and caused his death. No words can wash away that guilt.'

He stood up then and said, almost as though he was thinking the words he spoke rather than saying them, 'When I set forth on this journey, I did so because life at

Beauregard had grown irksome to me; I hated being penned in like a sheep. Also, I hated the thought that our father should bring another woman to the castle to take the place of our dear mother. And sometimes, as we have walked along the dusty road, tired and hungry, I have thought that I was a fool to leave a good home on such a wild goose chase as this. I have thought that if the going became too hard, we could always leave Stephen of Cloyes and return home, to ask father's pardon, and to live once more in comfort.' He paused a while, then said, 'But now there is no going back, until God has taken the guilt from my shoulders. Rightly or wrongly, the good priest of Lyons will have the officers out, searching for me and the stolen chalice. And rightly or wrongly, the relatives of the man I caused to die will want justice. From now, I must go on, to the Holy Land, to make my pilgrimage, to fight for the Holy Sepulchre. Only when that has been done can I return to France, to face whatever charge men wish to bring against me.'

Alys rose and put her arm about him. 'But, brother,' she said, 'all this guilt is in your own mind, not in the minds of others. Our father would see that justice was done to you, if we returned to Beauregard. Surely you know that?'

Geoffrey shook his head. 'It is easy for you to say that, Alys,' he said. 'But I am the one who stands at the centre of this trouble, and my heart tells me that I must make an act of expiation.'

The girl gave a sigh of exasperation and would have said more, to try to persuade her brother, but just then Stephen awoke and rubbed his tired eyes.

'Geoffrey of Beauregard,' he called, in his thick peasant's voice, 'stand at my right hand from now on. You are my friend and protector, my guide and my disciple. Come, Geoffrey, and break your fast with me, for soon we must take the road again.'

And Geoffrey took the hand of Alys and led her towards the wagon. 'Where I go, my sister goes, Stephen,' he said.

The boy prophet nodded his head gravely, and with a gesture of the hand indicated that they should both sit beside him in the straw.

'Aye, that is understood, dear friend,' he said. 'She, too, must be at my right hand when we enter the Holy City.'

14. *Nearing Marseilles*

THE march from Lyons to Marseilles was a hard one, though many small incidents occurred which, for a little while at least, took the mind away from hunger and thirst and growing weariness.

Once, for instance, they came upon a wandering showman who led a great brown bear, fastened by the snout to a staff. This bear danced clumsily to the rhythm which the man played on a little sheepskin tabor; but when the piper blew a gay gigue on his flute, the creature dragged itself away from the showman and seemed to lose its animal clumsiness, dancing on one leg, then the other, turning somersaults, even rolling itself up in a ball and trundling itself round in a great circle, near the piper's feet.

The showman looked astounded and offered the piper half-shares in all takings if he would join forces with himself and the bear; but the piper shook his head knowingly, and said, 'Nay, bear keeper, I go where there are better pickings to be had than thy bear can produce.'

All the same, the piper found it hard to get away, for the great bear seemed to have taken an immense fancy to him, and even tried to clasp him about the waist, so that he should not march away with the children.

And on another occasion, a troupe of tumblers walked with the children for a league or so and then offered Stephen a small bag of silver money if he would apprentice half a dozen of the smallest and lithest children to him.

Stephen refused, solemnly saying that he was not their father and could make no profit from their labours. The children laughed at this and willingly signed on with the tumblers, for by now they had had enough of walking to the Holy Land.

It was on this stretch of the journey that many other children left the great company, because of hunger and exhaustion. Some of them turned back and began the long journey towards their homes, once more; others stayed here and there in small towns or hamlets, where there was work for them, or where kind-hearted women, pitying their tired and ragged state, promised them a good home.

And, from time to time, there were those, mostly little ones, who fell sick and had to be left behind, for weak as they were for lack of food and sleep, they fell an easy prey to fevers in that unusually hot summer.

Sadly, many of them died, for lack of care. Even Stephen, whose heart was hardened by the fierceness of the flame of ambition that burnt within it, shed tears the morning he was called by one of his disciples to look at three small mites who had died in the night, and lay huddled together beneath a wild rose bush.

'In faith, my friends,' he said, 'these little ones are a sad memorial to our great mission. Our path through France might be followed in later years by those who care to seek out the little graves we leave behind us.'

It was a bad year, in the South of France, because of the great heat. Crops shrivelled and wells dried up. The villagers had nothing to spare; it was all they could do to feed their own children.

The great gay army of Stephen shrivelled too; and as they drew nearer and nearer Marseilles, more hangers-on attached themselves to the still great, though dwindling band – hedge-priests, without benefices, beggars, pickpockets, and such lawless rogues.

One night, when the lights of the Port of Marseilles were already within sight from the high ground where the children were encamped, Alys sat up with a start and clutched her brother.

'Listen,' she whispered, 'can you hear that bell?'

Geoffrey's face grew pale. 'I can hear it, sister, only too well. That is the bell of a leper. I pray God that he does not come among us, for we are in no condition to fight against such a disease, weak as we are with hunger.'

But the clanking of the bell passed by them, at a higher level of the hill, and all they heard as it passed was the thin and plaintive voice of the suffering beggar, as he rattled his wooden bowl.

'*Pour les pauvres! Pour les pauvres!*' it said. 'For the love of God, alms! Alms for a blind leper who cannot see the ground before him! Alms! Alms!'

Alys shuddered half in pity, half in terror; and the sound of that voice lived on in her memory all night.

But Geoffrey only said, 'Have courage, girl. Before we have finished our journey, we shall see many such. Perhaps we may even come to know what it is like to carry a bell and rattle a bowl.'

15. *Duel with the Sea*

THE next day they entered Marseilles, the piper stepping before them like a proud stallion, for all the world as though he led a merry bridal procession of folk who had eaten and drunk well for a week. Yet, in truth, many of the children by now were at the last point of exhaustion, and most of them were verminous and covered with sores.

But the air of the port was heavy with the exciting tang of salt and, for all their weariness, many of the children wished to run down the streets until they came to the sea, since, having come from inland France, they had never seen waves and breakers and foam.

However, Stephen called out to them imperiously, forbidding them to leave the great square where they were assembled until he had reminded them of their errand and had prayed God to bless their enterprise.

So they all knelt on the cobblestones, gazing at their leader as he stood erect in the wagon, telling how Moses had caused the Red Sea to divide, so that his followers, the children of Israel, might walk across, dry-shod, to the Holy Land. Then he went on to say that they, the children of France, should be no less blessed by God, but that very day should see the Mediterranean open when he, Stephen, commanded it to do so, as Moses had done before him.

As he spoke, on and on, some of the younger children found their attention wandering. ... White sea-birds swooped above their heads, against the deep blue of the Southern French sky; the tall and many-storeyed houses of Marseilles seemed to hang over the square, nodding their steeply gabled roofs, as though they intended to topple over, on to the cobblestones at any moment! And round about the edges of the square, on the pavements, crowds of people swarmed, to watch this strange gathering of wanderers.

There were men of all races who sail in and out of the harbours of the world, dark-skinned men who wore long black beards and ear-rings, some who dressed curiously in yellow robes and green turbans; knights in light armour, with their squires carrying their shields and pennants; chapmen, with trays of honey-cakes and coloured sweetmeats; lute players, who seemed always to be laughing in the sunshine; dancing girls with their shiny dark hair braided with gold, and gay ribbons floating from their shoulders; old men with grizzled heads, patches on their eyes, bent over sticks; young men, sitting upon their haunches gambling with dice; women carrying great baskets of bread; children spinning tops or blowing down whistles. . . . Oh, Marseilles was a merry, busy, devil-take-the-hindmost place, they thought, as Stephen's voice droned on!

'. . . and when, at last, we stand beside the sea, and I raise my right arm, and you see the angry waves cease in their lion-like conflict, and fall back, gentle as lambs, before our feet, then you will understand the will of God, which has led you forth from your homes, to drink from the cup of His Glory. And later, when we have walked the length and breadth of the Holy Land, setting it free once more, then you will know that I, simple shepherd lad of Cloyes, am the trusted emissary of the Most High Himself. . . .'

Suddenly a tall priest who stood in the crowd on the pavement called out, 'Have done, you petty blasphemer! Go back to your sheep, and tempt God's wrath no longer!' And as he spoke, as though by some arranged signal, the boys and youths, in that crowd about the square, began to pelt Stephen, and those nearest him, with refuse, laughing and jibing as they did so.

But Stephen did not budge, though his head and robe were bespattered, and at last, with a dignity far greater than many a Bishop might have commanded, he turned and led his vast procession down towards the harbour.

Alys had never seen a ship before, and when the many clustered masts, with their rigging and bright flags, came into view above the roofs of the nearest warehouses, she clapped her hands and danced.

'Oh, how exciting it is going to be!' she said.

But Geoffrey trudged on silently, his pale face set, as though there was some doubt in his mind, now that they had reached the end of the first stage of their pilgrimage.

So, followed by the folk of Marseilles, with drums beating, trumpets snarling, horses neighing and dogs barking, at last they stood the length of the long harbour, where the waves splashed lazily against the flanks of the moored, cargo vessels.

As Stephen climbed to the summit of a pile of wool bales, a great silence fell upon the assembled children, and a sea of white faces gazed towards him.

For a while, the boy seemed to commune with himself, staring up into the blue sky, as though praying. Then, for the space of a minute, a cloud seemed to come from nowhere, to obscure the bright sun and cast a shadow across the faces of the gathered multitude. Stephen seemed to shudder.

From the back of the watching crowd, the tall priest shouted, 'There, mountebank, you have God's warning! That is an omen, a sign of failure!'

The silence fell once again, like a heavy cloak, as Stephen gazed coldly upon the interrupter, his pale lips twisted into a smile of derision.

'My God has spoken to me,' he said. 'He will not betray me. I trust in Him now to make manifest His love for me.'

Here and there, among the crowd, girls and women sobbed, and one old woman laughed aloud, hysterical with the tension of the occasion.

Then Stephen turned to face the sea, his thin arms raised high above his head, until it seemed to some of the children that he was about to fly into the air, like a seabird, and leave them kneeling on the cobblestones of the harbourside.

He spoke once more to his followers, though his back was turned towards them, and his voice was now strong and full of faith.

'Close your eyes, my children,' he called in bell-like tones. 'Close your eyes and listen to my words, and, as you listen, pray for me. By God's good grace, when I tell you to open your eyes again, they will see the passage to the Holy Land, for the seas will have rolled back.'

Now, as all the children closed their eyes, Stephen signed himself and, in a voice of great authority, said loudly, 'In the name of God, in the name of Christian's faith, I command you, waters, to part so that we, the true Crusaders of the Holy Cross, may march to do God's work abroad!'

The waiting children heard the waves still beating against the moored vessels, the creaking of timbers, the straining of hempen rope. They heard the mocking cries of the seagulls over their heads.

Then Stephen's voice cried out again, now more impassioned than before, 'Hark, rebel waters, to my commandment while there is yet time. Roll back, I order you, or God will punish you and dry you up!'

Once more, the waiting children heard the sound of waves, of creaking timber, hemp, and wild sea birds.

Then from the back of the watching crowd of townsfolk, they heard the priest's high voice, laughing like a drunken man. A dog began to howl and then a woman cried out, half-laughing, half-weeping, 'Oh, the poor little one! The poor, poor little one!'

And, for the third time, Stephen spoke. 'My God,' he said, 'I pray you, do not forsake me now! Roll back the waves as you promised me in my dream, I beg you!'

'In his dream!' echoed the priest, laughing loud.

Then the laughter spread across the harbour like a great invincible wave, shattering itself on the high stone walls of all the warehouses, echoing among the cordage of the bouncing ships, to be thrown back at the kneeling children from the cruel beaks of all the circling gulls.

And they heard Stephen's broken voice shriek out, 'My God! My God! Why hast thou forsaken me?'

Then he began to cry, like the smallest one of all his followers, standing there, for all to see, on the bales of wool, his thin shoulders heaving, the tears running unchecked down his weary face.

And when the children opened their eyes, the sea was still there.

16. *Two Kind Merchants*

THEN, suddenly, a red-haired lad, wearing a ragged leather jerkin, stepped forward and clambered up on to the wool bales beside Stephen.

'My friends,' he called out, 'we have followed a fool! We have left our homes and our good folk only to be deceived by this fraud! Who will now follow me back? Come forward all those who despise this trickster, those who are willing to accept me as their leader, back to sanity and comfort!'

As these words echoed across the harbour, Stephen rose again, his hands out, imploringly. But the lad in the ragged jerkin struck out at him and Stephen went down, rolling to the cobblestones, all the power gone from him.

This was too much for Geoffrey. Two great strides carried him to where the red-haired youth stood laughing. He drew back his fist and punched the other as hard as he could.

'That's for you, coward!' he heard himself shout. Then the red-haired fellow rose and seemed for a moment as though he would leap at Geoffrey, but, seeing what manner of opponent faced him, thought better of it and, with a sneer, pushed his way through the crowd of children who now hemmed them in.

And as he went, many followed him, their faith in Stephen broken; yet many who had intended to desert the shepherd lad from Cloyes now stayed because of Geoffrey's stout action.

Alys had helped Stephen to his feet and tried to sponge away the blood from his nose. He looked back at her with a sad smile and said, 'I thank you, my lady. I am not worth your pity, though. Go with those who are turning to their homes, I beg you.'

Then the piper stepped forward and slapped Stephen on

the back. 'Cheer up, lad,' he said, smiling, 'every leader of men must learn what it is like to be despised by his followers. But the greatest leaders know that glory is not gained without a fight, and they press forward their attack even when all seems lost. Have courage, friend, and I promise you, you will yet live to see the Holy Land!'

Then he led Stephen and a few of the others to a tavern, where the vine leaves hung over the door, and bought them a meal of new white bread and veal cutlets.

Stephen's spirits rose a little after he had eaten, and he left his companions to pray in a little white church by the dockside.

Alys and Geoffrey walked in the town, wondering what they should do now, hoping that the piper's words might come true, yet hardly knowing how that could be.

Towards evening, they came to a little winding street, which circled round on itself up the hill, so that they could look down on the houses below. Alys suddenly stopped and pointed. 'Look who is there,' she said in a whisper.

Geoffrey followed her pointing finger and saw a small square garden, enclosed by high grey stone walls. In the garden, seated on a bench at a trestle-table laden with food and wine, sat the piper. Two other men sat with him, talking urgently in low voices. One of them was immensely fat, and wore a blue robe held in by a broad belt of gold. His short fingers glittered with rings. The other man was small and hunched, and seemed always to be laughing silently at some jest which only he knew of. His face was pale, his nose as hooked as the beak of a hawk. He wore a black patch over his left eye.

'Look,' said Alys suddenly, 'the piper is showing them the golden cup which he stole from the church!'

Geoffrey's anger rose now. 'So that is it!' he said. 'They must be money-lenders and the piper is the rogue we took him for, after all!'

Geoffrey strode back down the hill, his sister finding it hard to keep up with his angry steps. But when they reached the stone wall and went through the open gate into the little garden, his fury faded away at the piper's words.

'Geoffrey and Alys of Beauregard,' he said, placing his hands on their shoulders, as though they were the closest friends in the world, 'I want you to meet William "The Pig" and Hugh "The Iron".'

First the fat man, then the thin one, bowed as their names were spoken, though Alys thought they seemed annoyed

that the piper should have mentioned their rather uncomplimentary nicknames.

The piper went on. 'They are two merchants of Marseilles. They saw what happened this morning by the harbour-side and they feel sympathetic to poor Stephen, and to all of you who followed him.'

William 'The Pig' rolled his eyes and rubbed his beringed hands across his vast stomach.

'Alas, alas!' he said. 'Such a disaster would be insupportable, if there were not good Christian men left in the world to put such a sad situation to rights again!'

Hugh 'The Iron' nodded in agreement, his pale face seeming paler, by contrast with his great black patch.

'True! True!' he said. 'Praise be to God that we are both willing and able to help Stephen and his army of children towards their ambition.'

Geoffrey and his sister gazed at the two men, bewildered. But the piper, smiling, clapped them both on the shoulder.

'You can go back to the harbour, my friends, and tell poor Stephen that all is now well, for I have been able to arrange with these Christian gentlemen that you shall have your desires. You shall go to the Holy Land – but not on foot. William and Hugh, generous souls, have agreed to put seven good ships at your disposal and to carry you, without cost to any of you, to the Land of your hearts' desire!'

As the children gazed at the men in that little secluded garden, William 'The Pig' smiled again and rubbed his stomach.

'We are honoured to serve such as you,' he said.

'Aye, that we are,' echoed Hugh 'The Iron', his white face wrinkled into a grinning mask.

On the way down to the harbour, Alys said, 'This is fine news – but I do not like the looks of the two merchants, brother!'

Geoffrey strode on, anxious to be first to tell Stephen of the good fortune which had befallen them.

'You are only a girl, Alys,' he said breathlessly, 'and you do not understand the ways of the world. Consider how you misjudged the piper, good fellow that he is! Don't you understand now that he was paying for those ships with the golden chalice?'

Alys said doubtfully, 'Yes, but it was not his in the first place. He stole it from the church.'

Geoffrey clucked with impatience. 'There you are,' he said, 'just like a girl – you can't see further than your silly nose! The piper is acting as God's agent; he has borrowed something belonging to God so as to do God's will. That golden cup will get us to the Holy Land – indeed, it will be as though God Himself rolled back the sea! No one believes that prophecies will come to pass exactly according to the letter; one must interpret them, you see?'

Alys nodded. 'And you still think that William and Hugh are good men, in spite of their faces?'

Geoffrey laughed and tugged at her hair.

'Of course they are!' he said. 'They cannot help what their faces look like, and that doesn't matter. Their hearts are of gold!'

And then they reached the harbour and went in search of Stephen.

PART THREE

*

17. *Loss and Re-Union*

FOR three days they had waited on the shore, their eyes fixed on the horizon, wondering whether Stephen's promise would be broken again. And then the ships had come, bobbing about like top-heavy wagons, trundling rather than sailing into the harbour. Not the splendid ships they had seen in their dreams, certainly, but ships! Ships that would carry them to the Holy Land, after all.

And then the children had rushed forward, each wanting to be quite certain of a passage to glory, almost like an army in full charge, shouting, laughing, jostling each other without feeling or even mercy.

Many were hurt, some even fell into the littered waters of the harbour, to be fished out, spluttering and half-drowned, by the grim-faced sailors who manned the ships.

In all the confusion, Stephen, imploring the children to act like gentle lambs of God, had been pushed onwards, his shouts unheeded, into the first ship, the *Esperance*.

Then a terrible thing happened, something which brother and sister had feared in their nightmares.

In the tumultuous, swirling movement of the crowd, Alys could no longer hold on to Geoffrey's arm. He felt her grasp slacken, saw the agitated look in her wide eyes, even watched her mouth open as she shouted desperately to him. But so great was the hubbub about them, he heard no word come from her lips.

'Alys! Alys!' he yelled, grabbing out at her. 'Come back!' But his sister had gone, as though whirled away from him in some vast maelstrom, and he was left holding a piece of fabric, torn from the hem of her tunic.

Then in his turn, he was shoved, willy-nilly, towards the gangplank of the ship *Sancta Maria*. For an instant he became so confused and helpless and dizzy that he almost lost his balance and fell down into the black water which gurgled and slapped between the ship's side and the slimy green stones of the wharf.

He gave a sudden cry and keeled over, straining madly to stay on the plank as his companions pushed by him.

Then a strong hand clasped him by the arm, pulling him sideways, out of immediate danger.

Geoffrey turned, his heart thumping wildly with the sudden fear which had overwhelmed him, intending to thank his protector.

He looked into the face of Brother Gerard.

'Gerard!' he said. 'But where have you sprung from!'

The priest smiled back at him, ironically, and the boy saw that his face was grimed and pale, as though he too were weary.

'I have not sprung from anywhere, Geoffrey,' he said. 'In faith, I have not the strength left to spring at all! I have been all the time trying to find you, amid this multitude. I got into Marseilles only this morning, luckily for you, my friend!'

Then, as the crowd behind them pushed them on and on, into the swaying ship, Geoffrey said, 'Has father sent you to fetch us back?'

The priest shook his head. 'Your father has been in one of his strange moods. When he felt sure that you had marched with Stephen, he decided to let you go to Marseilles with Stephen, for he was certain you would return home, humble, when the sea did not open for you!'

'But he was mistaken', said Geoffrey. 'And now we have lost Alys as well. What can we do, Gerard?'

The priest shook his cropped head. 'I do not know,' he said, 'but we must have faith in God. I saw her being pulled from your side, but could not reach you in time to save her. I only know that she was swept aboard the third ship, the one with red patches in its sails. Please God, we shall find her when we land again. That is our only hope.'

Then, with the white gulls swirling low over their heads, and the clustered folk of Marseilles waving and laughing and shouting out after them, the *Sancta Maria* was pulled out into the harbour, and, catching the breeze in her dirty sails, wallowed after the other ships.

It was when they were fifty yards out, on the oily water, that Geoffrey looked back at the harbourside and, pointing, said almost in terror, 'But look! Look, Gerard, the piper has not sailed with us! He said he would lead us to the Holy Land – but he is standing laughing with the two merchants, William "The Pig" and Hugh "The Iron".'

The priest shaded his eyes and gazed to where the lad pointed. 'I see a fellow in a jester's habit,' he said. 'There is a fat man and another with a black patch over his eye. They are giving him something, it seems. It looks to be money, from the small leather bags in which it is contained!'

It was then that Geoffrey first realized the trap into which they had fallen; and when the Captain of the *Sancta Maria* came forward and threatened the children with a score of lashes if they did not obey him in all things, he had no doubt.

'Oh, what will happen to us!' sobbed a little girl, who stood near by.

The red-faced Captain heard her and turned, smiling wickedly. 'You'll have this old tub capsize, if you don't spread yourselves out evenly. That is what will happen to you, my girl!' he said.

18. *Storm and Treachery*

WHATEVER the ardours of the long and dispiriting march through France, those of the voyage were many times worse. Herded together like young cattle, the children suffered hunger, thirst, and sickness. By night they lay huddled in heaps on the filthy deck; by day they gathered round the bulwarks, gazing until their eyes hurt in the harsh sunlight towards the far horizon.

Most of the children suffered their privations almost gladly, thinking that Stephen's prophecy was being fulfilled, thinking too that their sufferings on the journey were planned by God to test their faith. Each curse from the rough seamen, each piece of mouldy black bread or dish of greasy soup, they regarded as a stepping-stone towards the state of sanctity. And even when any of their number were whipped by a too-hasty Captain, their fellows saw this as a necessary condition of their good fortune in being transported to the land of Heart's Desire.

Only those aboard the *Sancta Maria* had seen that the piper had deserted them, only they had seen money changing hands on the quayside, and had guessed what that indicated. And of these observers, Geoffrey and Gerard were perhaps the most acute.

'If I were alone, or if Alys were with me,' said Geoffrey one night, as the *Sancta Maria* headed due south, 'I would fling a plank overboard and leap after it. Someone would pick us up, surely?'

The young priest smiled grimly and then nodded. 'Yes,' he replied, 'other wolves, perhaps, as rapacious as these in whose care we now find ourselves. No there is no way, but to trust God and to go forward, wherever our pattern takes us.'

Then something happened which must have convinced

many of the hapless passengers that God had become displeased with them.

Some days out from Marseilles, a great storm blew up suddenly. Thunder roared like a thousand lions and lightning flashed so constantly and with such a blinding brilliance that it seemed like day, though it was midnight. The mast of one of the foremost ships was struck, and fell, cloven, with all its sails and cordage, upon the thickly clustered children who kneeled, praying beneath it.

Then a monstrous rushing wind came out of the west and blew the helpless ships off their course, heeling them over until the children could no longer keep their positions, but were rolled like bales or kegs this way and that, unable to help themselves.

The following morning as the storm blew itself out and as dawn broke beneath the leaden clouds, Geoffrey and Gerard, still clinging, though with numb fingers and pain-racked muscles, to the rigging, saw a sight which brought tears to their smarting eyes.

Two of the ships were no more. One lay, keel uppermost and shattered, on the rocks of a small island to the east. The other was settling slowly in deep water, its sails now floating idly on the wash, its many passengers scattered momentarily on the surface of the waters like seeds upon a pool.

Though they were a long distance away, Geoffrey thought he could hear many of them shouting for help. Then, singly or in groups, they disappeared before the nearest ship could manoeuvre itself in their direction.

Geoffrey fell to his knees, his hands over his eyes. 'I pray to God that these poor souls may yet be safe,' he said. Then, almost in the same breath, 'And I thank Him that the ship with the red patches on her sails is still afloat – that my sister, Alys, has not suffered the fate of those other poor little ones.'

The priest kneeled beside him, praying.

Then at last he said, 'We must have faith, my son. The

island upon which one of the ships ran is San Pietro, and the greater island which lies beyond it is Sardinia. There is every chance that the good folk of the island will rescue all they can.'

The next morning, word was shouted from one ship to the *Sancta Maria* that it was the *Esperance* that had foundered, and though Geoffrey was still relieved that his sister's ship had not suffered in the storm, the news that the *Esperance* was no more cast a heavy gloom upon him. For Stephen, their leader, had been aboard her.

Indeed, a rough-voiced sailor had shouted out that he had actually seen Stephen in the seas, refusing to grasp at ropes or planks flung to him, and praying in a loud clear voice all the time, until his water-sodden garments dragged him down. Now, to the children, it seemed that their pilgrimage was at an end, that there was nothing to go forward for. Yet when some of the stouter-hearted called out to the sailors to turn the *Sancta Maria* about, and set course again for Marseilles, all they received in reply were sneers and curses and blows. The Captain lounged forward then, swinging a knotted rope in his great hand.

'What's this about turning back?' he shouted. 'No, no, my pretty ones, you are too precious a cargo for that. You asked to go to the Holy Land, and, by Beelzebub and the nine furies, to the Holy Land you shall go, or Jean Gaspin isn't my name!'

A young farm lad from the Auvergne stepped forward then, his strong muscles tensed, his eyes wide with anger.

'It is our wish to turn back, Captain,' he said. 'Who are you to deny us? We are not slaves!'

With a brutal laugh, the Captain struck him to the deck. Geoffrey would have leaped at the Captain's throat then, in his anger, but Gerard restrained him.

'Have patience, my son,' he whispered. 'Are we not taught that God is aware even of a sparrow's fall?'

After that the children were like cowed dogs. Now, few of them had any hope left in their hearts.

And when at last they saw land rising ahead and coming forward to meet them, a shore on which clustered many white buildings, they felt no excitement.

And then, when a squadron of long low ships swept swiftly about them, manned by dark-skinned, black-bearded men, wearing brightly coloured robes and pointed shining helmets, they were not excited, only numb with apprehension.

'Well, my little cabbages,' called out the laughing Captain from the poop, 'here we are, safely in the Holy Land! The Port of Bougie lies ahead, the nicest little harbour in Algeria! And these fine black-bearded gentlemen, who have come out to welcome us, are Saracens, every one of them! Now how do you like the Holy Land, hey, my chickens?'

The lad from the Auvergne spat at him, his eyes ablaze.

'You traitor!' he said. 'You traitorous swine! May God punish you for this!'

For a while the Captain glared down at him, the veins standing knotted in his neck. Then he said slowly, for all to hear, 'If I did not wish to get a good price for you in the slave market, I would flay the skin from off your back, you midden-cock!'

Suddenly the lad gave a high cry and, pushing past his fellows, swung himself over the side and fell into the sea.

But he did not get far. A long Saracen galley pulled alongside him and he was dragged aboard, fighting and shouting.

Geoffrey turned to the priest, his face pale and set now. 'Perhaps those who went down with the *Esperance* were the lucky ones, after all,' he said.

But Brother Gerard shook his head and answered, 'Who are we to question God's will! Let us show what courage we have by facing what lies before us without flinching. There is as much courage to be shown by accepting one's fate, as there is in riding at a tournament.'

Then the *Sancta Maria* grated alongside the quay and a

score of shouting Saracens leapt aboard, carrying lengths of rope in their hands.

The ship's Captain waved down at them cheerfully, 'Welcome aboard, my merry lads,' he called. 'I told you I'd bring a rare cargo this time, didn't I? And when have you known Jean Gaspin to break his word?'

Geoffrey glared up at him and said through clenched teeth, 'One day, Jean Gaspin, I will be even with you, though I must live to be a hundred!'

He said no more, because he and Brother Gerard were pushed forward towards the gangplank, their hands tied tightly behind them.

19. *Abu Nazir*

THE slave-market of Bougie was a riot of colour beneath the dark blue African sky. Men and women moved about, dressed in brightly striped robes, golden ear-rings, and armbands glittering in the aching sunlight. The painfully white square buildings flung back the sun's heat and light against the eyes, until it was almost unbearable to look at them.

Here and there, under scores of red and blue awnings, the children stood or squatted, still tied, while dark-skinned merchants moved among them, selecting one, rejecting another, always smiling and nodding, as though they were at peace with the world, as though Saracen power would never crumble or its wealth grow less.

Geoffrey had been brought up to regard men with brown skins as being somehow inferior to those with white, the men he knew, knights like his father with fair or red hair, and a love of dogs and horses. And now a man with a deep brown skin approached him, staring down arrogantly upon him, surveying him from crown to toe with dark crafty eyes. The boy could sense that this man was rich; his turban was encircled with bands of twisted gold, his fingers were heavy with the same metal, while a thick silver-thread fringe flapped lazily at the hem of his brocade robe.

Yet when the man stretched out his hand to feel Geoffrey's muscles, the boy pulled away, almost in disgust. 'I am not a fat pig to be prodded!' he shouted. 'I am Geoffrey de Beauregard and a true Frenchman!'

The Saracen's hand stopped in mid-air. His head bowed slightly and with infinite grace. His dark eyes narrowed, so that there were wrinkles at their corners. His thin-lipped mouth twisted itself into a smile of immense amusement.

And when he spoke, it was in a French so pure, so well

articulated, that King Philip himself could not have equalled it.

'I am delighted to meet you, Geoffrey of Beauregard,' the Saracen said gently. 'I am Abu Nazir, once a soldier of some small fame, now a merchant among other things.'

The boy replied, 'I am not concerned with what you were, or what you are. A Saracen is a Saracen, whatever he chooses to call himself, just as a wolf is a wolf; nothing more!'

The man regarded Geoffrey solemnly for an instant, then

blew upon the finger-nails of his right hand and carefully polished them on his left forearm.

And when he had done this, he said quietly, 'Your father, Robert of Beauregard, with whom I have had the honour to break a lance on a number of occasions, always showed excellent manners, whatever the occasion. His son does not seem to be blessed with the same gifts.'

Now Geoffrey gazed with astonishment at the merchant. 'I beg your pardon, Saracen,' he said, as proudly as he could manage, 'I took you for less than what you are. Any man my father thinks worthy of fighting has a certain merit.'

Once more the merchant polished his finger-nails with meticulous care. Then he said, almost lazily, 'That little castle of yours at Beauregard – is it still as damp and draughty as it used to be? And the tapestry that your gentle Lady Mother was making, with her ladies, the one with huntsmen and hounds bounding across it – was it ever finished? I have often wondered.'

Now Geoffrey's mouth stopped trying to be proud, and fell open in blank amazement.

The Saracen laughed and patted him kindly on the shoulder.

'Do not look so much like a suckling-pig with an apple in its mouth at Rouen Fair!' he said. 'There is no magic in it. Once I lived in Cordova, and was a member of a mission which came to France. Your father did me the honour of entertaining me for a while. I have not forgotten him – or you. A squawking little bundle you were, in those days, and haven't improved since, it seems!'

Then, as Geoffrey gazed at him, speechless, the merchant began to move away, leaning heavily on his silver-mounted staff of ebony.

Suddenly the boy's heart was full of fear. 'Sir,' he called, 'I am... I am...'

And his tongue would carry him no further, such was his shame.

The Saracen turned back and said gently, 'I understand, Geoffrey of Beauregard. You need say no more. I shall buy you, whatever the price, if only because your Lady Mother thought so highly of you, you and the tapestry! I will also buy one other friend of yours, if there is one for whom you feel a special affection!'

He paused for a while, running his sharp eyes up and down Gerard, the priest, who stood behind Geoffrey but had remained silent.

'Preferably,' went on the Saracen, 'one who knows and can teach Latin and Greek, for I am instructed by my master, the Governor of Egypt, al-Kamil, Son of al-Adil, the Great

One, to bring back only those slaves who can be used as interpreters, teachers, and secretaries.'

Brother Gerard bowed his head humbly and said, 'I thank you, sir, for your consideration, but I must advise you that I am a priest, a Christian man. Much as I would wish to be by the side of my charge, Geoffrey of Beauregard, my faith forbids me to do so if, by so doing, I must forsake Christ and follow Mahomet.'

The Saracen turned towards him and smiled, musingly, until Brother Gerard's eyes dropped. Then he said lightly, 'Have no fear, priest. My master, al-Kamil, is a civilized person! It is not his wish to offend those who serve him. A happy slave is an efficient slave, Christian! Let us put it like that, and leave the conversation there. I shall give orders that you are both to be put aboard my ship tonight. There is no more to say.'

He had made two paces away from the friends when he paused once again, and turning said slyly, 'Oh, yes, there is something I omitted to say. Geoffrey of Beauregard, tonight you will be pleased you begged my pardon for your rudeness! Or, should I perhaps say, pleased that your mother once did me the kindness of broaching her best cask of wine in my entertainment!'

And then he was gone, among the crowds, and the two friends were left gazing after him in wonder.

20. *The Secret Room*

THAT day seemed endless. Geoffrey's mind swirled with the sort of confusion that is only experienced in a nightmare. His sister was lost ... Stephen was drowned ... his sister was lost ... Abu Nazir might be a good friend – but his sister was lost, and the seas had not opened as poor Stephen had promised. But above all, his sister was lost, and he should have protected her, as was his bounden duty. ...

Squatting by his side, under the sun-baked awning, Brother Gerard said consolingly, 'My friend, the ways of God are inscrutable to poor small creatures, such as you and I. You did your best to keep tight hold on the Lady Alys. You must not blame yourself for something which you had not the power to prevent. In my heart, I feel that your sister is in the care of God – and we can wish for no more. These are strange times, young friend, with men milling about hither and thither, and as many rogues as good men in the world, each anxious to pick a purse, spoil a reputation, or cut a throat. ... Let us be thankful we have so far encountered what good we have; for, assuredly, things might be even worse than they are. Have courage, lad!'

Geoffrey tried to put on a good face then, though in his heart he still blamed himself for the loss of his sister.

Then, in the late afternoon, something happened which drove even the thought of Alys from his mind. A fat man approached and stood looking down on Geoffrey and the priest. He was obviously very rich, judging by the material of his robe and by the many golden rings upon his podgy fingers; but his appearance, in spite of this richness, was repulsive. His eyes had the milky sheen of a sufferer from trachoma; his flesh hung, heavy-jowled, over the tight neck of his robe; he glistened with perspiration, even with the slight effort involved in stroking his long and straggling moustaches.

'How much do you ask for these poor cattle?' he called out to the slave-master, who sat behind the pair.

'They are already sold, O Beloved of Allah,' answered the dealer. 'Abu Nazir bought them earlier and will take them away this very evening. Let me show you two others, O Next-to-Divine One.'

The fat merchant snorted with disgust. 'No, No!' he shouted, 'I want these two. They suit my requirements. No others would do. I will not be bested by Abu Nazir – just because he was once a great warrior! Nay, by the beard of the Prophet, I will pay double what Abu Nazir gave for them. Come, slave dealer, accept my money and I will take them now.'

And with that, he flung a jingling leather bag at the man, smiling triumphantly as he did so.

Geoffrey saw, with something amounting to terror, that the greedy slave-dealer was about to accept this offer.

Then a very tall man pushed his way through the crowds about the booth, a man dressed, despite the day's heat, in chain mail. A great beak of a nose jutted forth beneath his high helmet. Black-bearded, his hand upon the golden hilt of his curved sword, he said, 'What is this, O pig of a slave-dealer? Do you betray my master, Abu Nazir, to the first fat dog that ambles along with a better offer?'

The slave-dealer flung down the bag of gold and fell to his knees, gibbering, 'O, Tiger among men, I swear I did not mean to sell these slaves again! I swear it, by the beard of the Prophet!'

The warrior smiled down in contempt at the fellow, then pushed him sprawling with his mailed foot.

The fat merchant spluttered with hurt pride and indignation. 'I am no dog, assassin!' he shouted. 'I am Ala Zamara, the richest man in Bougie.'

The man with the black beard turned round on him slowly and with infinite contempt said, 'Then, Ala Zamara, you are not a fat dog. No, you are a fat pig! And if you do not trot away to your sty by the time I have counted ten, I will forget my vows and soil my good sword on your greasy carcase! Aye, four cuts will I make! This way! And then that! And the outcast dogs of Bougie shall be thankful for the feast I shall provide for them! Now go!'

Geoffrey laughed to see the fat merchant waddling away, waving his arms in fury.

But the Saracen bent down, his face now grave. 'Come, Frankish lad,' he said. 'In spite of my brave words, Ala Zamara is a powerful man. Inside a few minutes he will be back with his horde of hangers-on; he will try to take you by force. And, have no doubt, he will not be satisfied until my own head is on a pike about his palace, for the shame I have brought on him in this public market. Come with me, we must hide until my master is ready to sail tonight.'

The two followed the tall Saracen into a narrow alleyway behind the slave market, where the tall white houses seemed to lean over and almost touch, leaving only a narrow strip of burning blue sky above them. Half-way down this street, the Saracen knocked on a blue-painted door, which was opened almost immediately by a dark-eyed girl, who bowed her head when she saw who her visitor was.

'Hurry, woman, and bolt the door,' said the Saracen. 'We have incurred the enmity of the greasy pig, Ala Zamara, and I have no wish to leave my body on your doorstep.'

The girl stood aside to let them mount the narrow marble stairs that led upwards to a circular landing.

'You know your way, warrior chief of Abu Nazir. The secret room is at your disposal.'

'Thank you,' replied the Saracen. 'Bring food and drink, for these poor devils are hungry and thirsty.'

'Your slightest wish is my iron law,' whispered the girl, as she hurried away.

The secret room had a ceiling so low that the Saracen could hardly stand upright in it. Most of the floor space was taken up by a great square bed, on which they all sat.

The wall opposite the door contained an unglazed lattice window which ran almost its whole length and which looked down on a small square courtyard, half-filled with hay and cow dung. In the oppressive heat of the afternoon, flies swarmed about the window. Geoffrey passed his hand over his damp forehead.

'By Saint Michel,' he said, 'but I have smelled sweeter air than this.'

The Saracen looked at him darkly. 'Beggars cannot be choosers,' he said. 'And do not forget, boy, that you are now a slave. A slave has no finer feelings.'

Then, amused by the indignant expression on Geoffrey's face, he laughed aloud and added, 'Or, I should say, he does not show them, if he is a good slave.'

Geoffrey said hotly, 'I am a freeborn Frank. I am no slave.'

The Saracen whistled a little tune and then said quietly, 'Which of us is free, when all comes to all? We call ourselves free, but free to do what? Free only to do what Allah commands.'

Brother Gerard half rose and was about to join the argument, when the door opened and the girl entered, bearing a tray on which stood a dish of honey cakes and three goblets of a light red wine. The Saracen gave her a coin and, after bowing her head, she left them.

Geoffrey, whose thirst was by now great, was about to drain his goblet when the Saracen suddenly gripped him by the wrist.

'Do not drink,' he said mysteriously. Then he began to sniff his own wine like a keen-scented hound, following its quarry.

'So that's the game, is it!' he said, and flung his wine through the window, into the courtyard.

Then, turning to the other two, he said, 'That wine is drugged. There is about it a faint aroma which comes from the herb from which the poison is squeezed. This woman would hand us over, helpless, to the fat pig, Ala

Zamara; of that there is no doubt. My master shall hear of this – and when he does, I would not be that woman!'

He had hardly finished speaking when there was shouting at the bottom of the stairwell, followed by the sounds of many feet as they rushed upwards.

The Saracen looked at the flimsy door with contempt. 'That will not keep them out for long,' he said. 'Help me to move this bed against the door. It may give us a few seconds more in which to say our last prayers!'

When they had done this, he drew his curved sword and slashed at the lattice of the window until he had made space enough for them to pass through.

'Come, friends,' he said, 'let us see if we can fly! They say even that is possible, if only one has faith great enough!'

Once more, Brother Gerard was about to speak sternly to him for taking such a matter so lightly; but Geoffrey clapped the priest on the shoulder and said, 'At least we shall have something soft to land on!'

Then, even as the knocking began on the flimsy door, the three clambered up to the window and leapt.

21. 'Run Now, if You Wish to Live!'

It was while he was in mid-air that Geoffrey saw the gate to the courtyard open and a group of green-turbaned men rush in among the straw.

'Up, Beauregard!' he yelled, even as he landed, and ran at them, his fists flailing. Beside him loped Brother Gerard, his narrow jaw set, his usually mild eyes now aflame with excitement. Somewhere behind them ran the Saracen. They did not see him, but heard the harsh war cry that burst from his bearded throat: 'Allah-il-Allah!'

Then the world, for Geoffrey, suddenly became a frenzied flailing of arms and legs. He butted a great negro in the stomach and heard the man's grunt of surprise. He saw Brother Gerard swing a most unpriestly fist under the jaw of a pale-skinned Berber, whose eyes rolled back as he slumped to the straw.

Then Geoffrey heard a vicious swishing sound, somewhere above his head, and a man's high scream of pain. And when the boy's sight cleared again, he saw that the Saracen's sword blade glinted red, and that the ruffians had leapt aside to let him pass.

'Run now, if you wish to live!' growled the Saracen. They needed no second bidding, but turned out of the gate and into a narrow cobbled lane that led down towards the harbour. Behind them, Geoffrey still heard the sounds made by the wounded man.

'That hawk will not peck again,' said the Saracen, wiping his long sword as he ran.

Then suddenly the air was full of a strange whirring, as though a nest of hornets was in close pursuit of the fugitives. For a moment Geoffrey's bemused senses did not take in the reality of what was happening; then, before him on the cobbled road, he saw an arrow strike, break into two pieces, and rattle away along the lane.

And at the same time, Brother Gerard, who was running beside him, gave a deep gasp and stumbled to his knees.

'I am hit, Geoffrey,' he said. 'Run on. Do not let them take you. God will . . .'

Then his voice failed him and he sprawled his length, the feathered flight of an arrow showing beneath his left shoulder-blade.

Geoffrey bent over him, shocked that his friend should have been struck in the very moment of escape. But the Saracen brushed him roughly aside.

'You heard what I said,' he shouted roughly. 'Run if you wish to live. These men are not playing Blind Man's Buff!'

Then, as though Brother Gerard had been a small child, the Saracen swung him up over his shoulder and ran on.

'My master bought two slaves,' he grunted, grimly, 'and two slaves he shall have, even though one of them may not be worth much now!'

Geoffrey did not know whether to hate the man for his hardness, or to admire him for his warrior-like sternness and grim humour.

And then they rounded a corner and almost ran into a group of tall black-bearded men, in chain mail, who sat on the bollards of a little jetty, casting dice and laughing at each other's jokes.

'Why, look who comes here!' one of them called.

'It is Jebel Kamal himself! And carrying a Christian, by Allah! Welcome, Captain! And since when have you been a porter?'

The Saracen ignored their laughter, but laid Brother Gerard down as gently as if he had been a little child.

'This is no time for jesting,' he said. 'The fat pig, Ala Zamara, has a score of jackals up the hill who would be a better target for your wit!'

A big-chested man, whose hooked nose was broken across the bridge, giving him the expression of a furious eagle, yawned and said, 'A score of Ala Zamara's creatures, eh? Well, not more than three of us need go up to meet them!'

And then he drew his sword, a curved scimitar, much hacked about the edge, and turning he pointed at two of the others. 'You, my brother, Zen Abbas, and you, my cousin, Zarif Ben, come with me. We will teach these jackals how men fight!'

The three men ran from the jetty, then were lost to sight as they turned the corner.

Then the Saracen leader, Jebel Kamal, called out, 'Fetch the physician. There is work here that needs his skill – and perhaps more than his skill, for this shaft has struck shrewdly.'

Brother Gerard's pale face twisted into a wry smile.

'I would guess that your physician will have his work cut out to save me, Saracen,' he whispered. 'But have no fears for me, my spirit is at peace.'

Jebel Kamal looked down at him strangely. Then, swallowing hard, he said, 'Priest, you are a man, and a true man at that. I have known many great warriors who have lacked your fortitude. I salute you!'

Brother Gerard signed himself slowly, almost lazily, it seemed, though Geoffrey, who gazed at him with wet eyes, could see that the movement cost him great effort and pain.

'Oh, I don't know,' said Brother Gerard. 'No Christian makes a song and dance about a small scratch like this.'

Then his head fell and Geoffrey saw that he had fainted.

The Saracen, Jebel Kamal, took off his own fine cloak and, rolling it up, slipped it gently beneath Brother Gerard's head.

'If this man dies,' he said, as though to himself, 'I swear by the beard of the Prophet I will go back up the hill and take the head off the fat pig, Ala Zamara, with my own hands.'

The white-bearded physician was already on his knees, using scalpel and salve, lotions and bandages. After a while he rose and wiped his hands.

'You will not need to soil your sword on Ala Zamara's neck, Jebel Kamal,' he said. 'This man has a constitution like Mahomet Himself – he will live!'

Then Geoffrey almost burst into tears with joy, and as he looked up into the Saracen's eyes, he saw that they too were moist.

Shortly afterwards the three Saracens who had gone up the hill returned, still laughing as they wiped their swords. Their leader, the man with the broken nose, held up two hands. 'We accounted for so many,' he called, 'and not a scratch on any of us.'

Jebel Kamal turned away from him, shrugging his shoulders. 'They were bullocks, not bulls, my friend,' he snorted. 'Why, this boy could have done as well!'

But Geoffrey could see that he was jesting to hide his real feelings. And so could the warrior with the broken nose, who shrugged his broad shoulders and began to sing a little song, nonchalantly, as though he had not a care in the world.

A few minutes later, a long low boat swept towards the jetty, its prow heavily gilded, its sails of brightly striped silk.

'At last,' called Jebel Kamal, 'our master's boat is ready to take us on our way.'

Geoffrey gazed down at the swift ship, and his eyes almost jumped from his head. Seated in the shade of the stern was a group of boys and girls, slaves like himself, no doubt.

And in their midst sat his sister, Alys, laughing and waving up at him as though she were a peasant's daughter, going for a ride on a hay wagon.

'*Grâce a Dieu!*' called Geoffrey. 'I never thought I should be thanking God for your safety – but I am!'

PART FOUR

*

22. Audience with Al-Kamil

THE great house of al-Kamil at Damietta was a place of rest after the long voyage from Bougie. Brother Gerard sat with Alys and Geoffrey beside the ornamental fountain of white alabaster in the great courtyard, and together they recalled the adventures that had befallen them on the way.

Two days out from Bougie a Frankish ship had appeared from nowhere, trying to run across their bows to stop them, and, when the Saracen oarsmen had bent their backs like demons to avoid a boarding, had sent flight after flight of arrows after them. Jebel Kamal had stood up, amid the deadly hail, shouting abuse at the Franks. By some miracle, he was not hit, though the bulwark against which he leaned was suddenly thick with quivering arrows.

Abu Nazir had laughed and said, 'Sit down, man, and say your prayers! The devil will not go on protecting you!' Geoffrey had been impressed by the bravery of the Saracens in this affair. Always, back at home in Beauregard, the men freshly back from crusading had spoken of them as 'black-faced cowards'; but now the boy was seeing them in a new light. For a start, few of the Saracens he had met had black faces. Indeed, they were little darker in colour than many French peasants, who spent their days in the Provençal sun, harvesting; and, as for being cowards, well, such men as Jebel Kamal and Abu Nazir himself seemed the equal of most of the knights who had hunted or jousted at Beauregard.

As for Alys, her time had been spent in looking after Brother Gerard, washing his wound, applying fresh salve, changing his dressings. And always, as day followed day, the young priest seemed to get better and better in health. His eyes became brighter, his cheeks took on a ruddier colour, he joked more and more. The Arab physician, who sailed with them, had smiled and said, 'If His Eminence, al-Kamil, should ever wish to be rid of you, slave-girl, I will take you on as my apprentice, for it seems that your fingers have a healing magic in them.'

Alys had felt proud at this compliment, though she did not care to be addressed as 'slave-girl'. Geoffrey had merely laughed for, as yet, it had not fully dawned on him that he, too, was no longer free to ride and hunt as he wished.

And now they were in the courtyard, at Damietta, with the water splashing above them and the late summer sun striking up into their faces from the glazed tiles.

Abu Nazir had been kind to them during the voyage, and had promised that as soon as it could be arranged, he would personally introduce them to al-Kamil, the Egyptian Governor, who might be pleased to employ them in ways suited to their capabilities.

So they awaited the summons, and, as they sat together by the fountain, a troop of Saracen horsemen passed through the courtyard mounted on fine Arab horses which made Geoffrey's eyes start wide with wonder at their grace of movement and the pride of their bearing.

Jebel Kamal rode at the head of the troop, his hooked nose jutting insolently from beneath his shining helmet, his curved sword lying across his knees. Behind him cantered a score of warriors, bearded and arrogant, their eyes heavy-lidded and contemptuous.

But as the troop passed the fountain, the leader, Jebel Kamal, half-turned his head towards Brother Gerard, and raised his right hand in recognition. Then they passed on, out of sight, beneath a great white archway.

'That savage has certain admirable qualities,' said the priest, with a smile.

Geoffrey grinned. 'Yes,' he said, 'and one of them is the strength to carry you on his back out of danger.'

Brother Gerard flushed, then nodded. 'That is a debt which I can never repay,' he said simply. 'I cannot imagine myself with Jebel Kamal dangling over my shoulder!'

The children laughed at the picture which the priest's words brought up in their minds; then a yellow-robed official approached them, tapping the tiled pavement importantly with an ivory-headed wand. In perfectly articulated French, he bade them follow him to where al-Kamil awaited them.

Al-Kamil, Governor of Egypt, sat on a pile of silken cushions, contemplating a scroll of parchment. He was a slightly built man, with mild features and large doe-like eyes. His fingers were extraordinarily long and slender, his skin no darker than that of Geoffrey himself.

For a moment or two he surveyed the three friends, stroking his long thin moustaches. Then he said softly, 'Abu Nazir has spoken well of you and of your family. I need interpreters, teachers, and secretaries, folk of decent birth, like yourselves. Their work will be largely in French and in Latin. Are you three competent in those languages?'

Gerard, the priest, said gravely, 'French is our language, lord. As for Latin, this girl and I are competent; but my young master, Geoffrey of Beauregard, I am afraid, is abler at falconry than at his verbs and declensions! He makes up for this by a knowledge, far surpassing ours, of Provençal songs.'

Al-Kamil glanced searchingly at the priest, then at Geoffrey; then, passing the roll of parchment to the boy, he said, 'Have the goodness to translate this letter, from Pope Innocent to my Brother, al-Muazzam. You may omit the salutations and begin with the text.'

Geoffrey took the parchment with shaking hands and stared at the crabbed writing. For a moment the black ink letters seemed to swim and merge together. Then the boy blinked and said, 'Sir, I have no idea what this may be about. If I were a lord in my own castle, I should ring a bell and call my secretary to me. Then he would read this gib-

berish and tell me, in good honest French, what it was all
about.'

With a slight bow he handed back the parchment. For a
while al-Kamil looked at the lad, his mouth down at the
corners. Then he said, 'In a way, an honest answer; but, alas,
my young friend, you are not a lord in your castle, you are
a slave, begging a favour. And even if you were a lord in
your castle, it would be a wise and politic thing to be able
to read a letter such as this. Suppose your secretary were
untrustworthy? You would need to be able to check what
he had told you.'

Geoffrey said casually, 'If my secretary betrayed me, I
should have him whipped. That is all there is to it.'

As he spoke, he heard Brother Gerard clucking with annoyance behind him. Then al-Kamil said softly, 'You are
like so many Frenchmen – honest at heart, but stupid. No,
my boy, I fear that I cannot employ you as a secretary. You
shall be a gardener's boy, while your sister and the priest
here perform more learned tasks. We shall leave for my
palace in Cairo tomorrow since Damietta is a little too open
to attacks from any stray shipload of Templars with a mind
to make nuisances of themselves. Report to Abu Nazir, and
obey him in all things. Go, the audience is ended.'

23. Little Prince

But al-Kamil's plans were not to be fulfilled so easily. Even as the party made its way across the broad courtyard, they heard the high screaming of horns, the shouting of many men, and then the clanging of the great gates that protected the fortress on the banks of the Nile.

The troop of Saracen horsemen, which had cantered out so proudly but an hour before, now galloped back to safety – but with a difference. Half of the horsemen were wounded, some of the horses were riderless; and Jebel Kamal, the leader, he who had seemed so strong, so careless of his fate, lay across the painted saddle of his charger, dead.

As the iron-bound gates clashed shut once more, the first of the horsemen called out, 'We were ambushed! The Franks have brought their small ships up the river, past the chains, and are coming to attack us!'

In the disorder that followed, Geoffrey whispered to his sister, 'Saint Michel be praised! Now we may fall into the hands of our own folk once again, and escape from this slavery.'

But Alys turned on him a gaze so cold and distant that he was puzzled by the change in her appearance.

'Have you considered, dear brother,' she said scornfully, 'what you are saying? The men who are attacking Damietta are not likely to show us any more mercy than they have shown the riders who galloped in so recently. In the heat of battle, they will not stop to ask us if we are French or Egyptians. They will kill all before them – and boast of it afterwards in their draughty halls.'

Slowly Geoffrey answered, 'I do declare, Alys, you are more than half a Saracen yourself!'

'I always thought that boys were born fools,' she replied, 'and now I know that to be true. Consider, my sweet innocent, the treatment we have so far received since leaving Beauregard. ... A French piper led us into the hands of two French merchants; and they sold us into slavery at Bougie. It was left to a Saracen to buy us, Abu Nazir. Did he treat us badly? It was left to an Arab physician to heal Brother Gerard. And it was left to poor Jebel Kamal to rescue you when you were in difficulties. What have our folk done for us in comparison to that?'

Brother Gerard had overheard this conversation and remarked drily, 'There is good, and evil, in all men, whatever the colour of their skins. We shall be well advised to await the outcome of this attack before we pass judgement on any man.'

The outcome was not long to await. Armoured Saracens ran across the courtyard, sweeping all aside, carrying sheaves of arrows, dragging a great siege engine which flung balls of flaming pitch, and a cart full of stones which could be dropped from the battlements of the fortress upon the heads of all besiegers. They were followed by slaves, with braziers of fire.

'This has all the appearance of an amusing episode,' said Geoffrey, putting on a smile which perhaps belied his true feelings. Alys gave him an angry glance; then they were shepherded away from the walls of Damietta by an old and fussy grey-bearded steward with a long ebony staff which he knew how to use on the shoulders of any slave who did not obey him immediately.

But there was nothing amusing in the scenes that followed. Suddenly the courtyard was filled with death. Men fell with arrows in their chest, or lay groaning on the mosaic pavement with broken limbs. The great gates shuddered again and again with the blows of the battering rams that were being used on them by the besieging crusaders.

Once the air was full of fire-arrows, and the children crouched in the shadow of a great buttress so as not to be hit.

Later, rocks, as heavy as Geoffrey himself, hurtled over the walls and fell upon the courtyard, bounding again and again, like live things, across the open space, smashing the delicate tile-work, shattering the fountains, crushing anyone who stood in their path.

Alys said coldly to her brother, 'Now do you still believe that the Franks will pay any attention to such a small thing as you are?'

Geoffrey did not answer his sister this time, but looked away from the scene of carnage that unfolded itself before their eyes.

It was at this point that something happened which the children were to recall with excitement for many years to come. Out of the domed door of the palace ran a young boy, of eight years or so, exquisitely accoutred in silver chain mail, and wearing the high spiked silver helmet of a Saracen of good family. In his hand he bore a gleaming curved sabre; his young face was alight with excitement, and he seemed to be shouting a war cry as he ran in the direction of the walls.

One of the slaves called out, 'That is al-Fuazzem the little eagle, the son of al-Kamil himself!'

Geoffrey, who crouched with the others in the shelter of a broad buttress said, 'Only a prince would carry such a sword. He is a lucky one, that little Saracen!'

Even as he spoke, a great boulder, flung from a siege catapult beyond the wall, crashed down upon the courtyard and then bounded in its headlong rush across the shattered tiles. Brother Gerard saw before any of the others that the little prince stood in the path of this bone-crushing missile, and, even as a cry of concern rose about him, flung himself forward towards al-Fuazzem. The small boy was flung sideways with the impact of the priest's body, and both of them rolled as helplessly as rag dolls out of the path of the bouncing stone.

Suddenly, as court officials appeared from nowhere, to surround them, the little prince looked up and said in perfectly articulated French, 'Who are you, Dog, who dares to treat me so? Know you not whose son I am?'

'Little Prince,' he said, 'in the face of death nobility knows no privilege. Here is your sword.'

But a bearded courtier snatched the weapon from the hand of the priest and said curtly, 'Such as he may not accept a favour from the hand of an unbeliever. Go back to your place, slave. It is well that the prince suffered no harm.'

But an hour later, when the attack had been beaten off and the fort was quiet once again, the same courtier came to Brother Gerard and said with a smile, 'We are all apt to speak unkindly when the air is full of arrows. Have the goodness to follow me, slave. You will find that the little prince is not ungenerous.'

Once more the priest stood before al-Kamil, the Governor; and this time the little eagle, al-Fuazzem was there also, sitting upon a great brocaded cushion at his father's right hand.

Al-Kamil said gently, 'For a Christian, you seem to be a good man, priest. You have saved my son's life, and for that I am indebted to you.'

Brother Gerard's thin face was creased in a smile for a moment, then he answered, 'I have paid my debt, al-Kamil; an Arab physician saved my own life at Bougie when first I was sold into slavery. Now we are even.'

For a while al-Kamil sat, smoothing his long moustaches, nodding his fine head as though he contemplated some problem in mathematics or science. Then he looked up and said lightly, 'Integrity is a fine virtue, my friend. It seems that we Muslims are not the only possessors of it. But where it is found, it should be rewarded. Priest, you are a free man to go where you will. Say the word, and I will have you put ashore wherever there are Christian knights to tend to you.'

But Brother Gerard shook his head gently and smiled.

'Sir,' he answered, 'I am not a free agent, to please myself what I do or where I go. My worldly master is the Sieur de Beauregard, whose priest I am, and whose family I serve.

My master's children are your slaves and I must stay with them in slavery to do what I may for them. So I must refuse your well-meant offer, though I thank you for making it.'

Al-Kamil turned to his little son and said, 'You are old enough now to study Latin, my child. Will you take this man as your tutor?'

Al-Fuazzem smiled and bowed his head with a dignity out of all measure for one of his age.

'I like the Frankish priest, father,' he said. 'With him, I shall learn much.'

Al-Kamil turned back to Brother Gerard and said, 'That is the answer, priest. You will assume the dignity of a free man once more and become my son's personal servant. Do you agree to that?'

Brother Gerard smiled and answered, 'It seems to be God's will that this should be so. I shall not contest it.'

As he went to the door, al-Kamil called after him, 'The two children you have mentioned, the son and daughter of your master, they shall be treated well. You will not be separated from them, that I can promise you.'

Outside in the long white corridor, Abu Nazir waited, pacing up and down. When he saw the priest, he went forward and clapped his hand on his shoulder.

'I am glad that things have turned out so well,' he said. 'Now come with me and we will find you more appropriate garments for the tutor of a prince. These rags you wear are in great need of a rest! And we must travel south to Cairo at dawn.'

Brother Gerard said tiredly, 'Thank you, but these rags, as you call them, are my bounden uniform, my livery of Christ. I should wear them even if I were forced to serve an Emperor, much less a mere princeling. If you have clothes to spare, give them to Alys de Beauregard; she would no doubt appreciate them more than I do.'

Abu Nazir replied, 'As you will, priest. I shall see that she and her brother are looked after, and when you change your mind, let me know and then the finest robe of silk shall be yours for the asking. That is the command of al-Kamil himself. He is not unmindful of the debt he owes you.'

Brother Gerard merely nodded and then went across the ruined courtyard to tell Geoffrey and Alys of his change of fortune.

24. Geoffrey in the Garden

THE river-trip to Cairo had been an uneventful one, and now the royal party sat under gay awnings in a hanging garden above the courtyard. They had been in Cairo a week.

Brother Gerard was painstakingly drilling the little prince in Latin grammar, while Alys was showing a young girl, the daughter of a courtier, how one laid out an embroidery pattern on a tambour.

Below, in the courtyard, Geoffrey, now dressed in a coarse robe of brown linen, followed an old and ill-tempered gardener from flower-box to flower-box, trying to learn how one tended the blooms. Already he had picked up enough Arabic to understand simple statements and to express himself, though crudely, with some force.

The old man said suddenly, 'By the beard of the Prophet, but I could teach a lame dog to cut flowers more easily than I can teach you, O Son of an Unbeliever!'

Geoffrey stared back at him, boldly, unlike the other slave boys, who went in fear of the cross old fellow. This annoyed the gardener.

'Look!' he shouted. 'You have broken the stems of three flowers already this morning. An example must be made of you!'

Geoffrey gazed back at him and said quietly, 'If you touch me with that stick, I will put you into that cistern and hold you there until you beg for mercy.'

The gardener had never been spoken to before in this manner. His dark eyes almost popped out of his head; his thick grey beard bristled with rage. Then, almost unable to control his mounting anger, he turned and called to the many slaves who clustered round him, 'Hey, you fellows, teach this dog a lesson. I order you to beat him soundly and then to throw *him* into the cistern. You shall each receive an extra ration of meat in this evening's meal.'

Alys looked up from her embroidery at the shouting that rose from the flower-beds below. She hastened to the marble balustrade to find out the cause of the uproar. Gerard and the prince, al-Fuazzem, stood beside her.

His back against an ornate gilded pedestal, Geoffrey was punching out right and left, sending slave after slave sprawling, while the angry gardener, waving his stick in the air, stood in the rear, threatening all and sundry with a fearful vengeance if they did not punish this wild Frank immediately and throw him into the water.

Alys watched her brother for a moment and then said, 'I must go down to help him, Brother Gerard. It is not fair, ten on to one.'

Brother Gerard held her arm and said, 'Stay where you are, my lady. Geoffrey seems to know well enough how to protect himself – and there is little point in your becoming involved in what, after all, is an affair of men and not of gentlewomen!'

'How he can fight!' said the prince, al-Fuazzem. 'I wish I might be down there with him. We would make short work of that rabble!'

Brother Gerard smiled at the boy but said nothing.

Just then, Geoffrey gave a great shout of 'Up Beauregard! Death to the infidel!' And, putting his head down, he bundled his way like an enraged bull. The slaves parted before him. Geoffrey's head caught the angry gardener in the midriff and the man rolled over and over, on the marble pavement, gasping and clutching his stomach.

The little prince jumped with joy and called out, 'That's the way, Frank! That was a good trick! Now knock some more of them over!'

But Geoffrey, panting with his exertion, was prevented from carrying out this suggestion, for a party of steel-helmeted guards, their javelins pointed towards his heart, had surrounded him.

'Fasten him in the deepest dungeon!' howled the gardener, now sitting up and rubbing his stomach.

'Later I will have him flogged publicly. All slaves must know what will happen to them if they disobey me!'

But the guards ignored the old man, and their leader, a smiling young officer whose face bore the signs of many battles, said in the *lingua franca* that had been evolved over the years, between Saracen and Frank, 'Geoffrey of Beauregard, you have the makings of a good fighter – but this was hardly the place to demonstrate your talents! Al-Kamil is strict with slaves who do not know their place. Come on, now, and do not attempt any more of those berserk charges. We are not slaves and aged gardeners!'

Alys started forward with dismay as she saw her brother being marched out of the courtyard, towards the royal palace of al-Kamil. Even Brother Gerard, usually so philosophical about life, looked crestfallen.

And when they turned to find al-Fuazzem, the little prince had gone, leaving his Latin book on the sun-scorched marble floor, as though he had now lost all interest in that branch of learning.

25. Change of Fortune

GEOFFREY stood before al-Kamil, his arms and legs still trembling with the effort of the fight he had put up in the courtyard. Al-Kamil's pale face was set and inscrutable.

'Are French boys in the habit of knocking down old men?' he asked drily. 'Old men who cannot defend themselves?' he added, his lips twisting a little scornfully as he spoke.

Geoffrey's mouth was bleeding, from a chance blow by one of the gardener's boys. His knuckles were grazed from the many hits he had scored in the tussle.

He answered as controlledly as he could, 'Sir, the old man, about whose welfare you are concerned, should by now have learned wisdom. He should know that it is unwise to threaten a person of quality with a stick.'

Al-Kamil gazed through him for a long while, until even the guards began to feel a sort of embarrassment creeping over them. Then he spoke at last.

'My gardener is my servant,' he said. 'You are my slave. The one I pay for his services; the other I have bought with good money, as one might buy a dog, or a monkey, or a wooden bowl. Who are you, then, to speak to me of wisdom, of persons of quality?'

The boy bit back the angry reply which had already reached his bruised lips. Then, with as courtly a bow of the head as he could manage, he said quietly and gravely, 'Sir, whatever you may say, I regard myself as a free man, subject only to the commands of God, my father, and the King. I am not anxious to spend the rest of my life as a gardener's boy, dressed in sacking. Therefore, I make this one request of you: give me a sword and turn me loose in the courtyard with any of the soldiers here. I promise you that you will not doubt my quality after that.

And I, for my part, would as soon die at the end of a Saracen sword, as live under the everlasting threat of a Saracen whip.'

The guards shifted uneasily as the boy spoke. Then al-Kamil stilled them with a swift glance as he replied, 'You are a fool, but a brave fool. Yet you are still a slave, my young friend; remember that.'

Then suddenly he made a small gesture with his right hand, as though waving the soldiers from his presence. Their leader saluted smartly and turned to the door, followed by the others.

Geoffrey stood alone, facing al-Kamil for a while, in a silence that was almost tangible.

Then an inner door swung open and the little prince came forward, followed closely by Abu Nazir. Geoffrey saw that they were all smiling now.

'Well,' said al-Kamil, shrugging his shoulders as though he was no longer responsible for the course he was about to take, 'you have heard what this young berserk has said, Abu Nazir?'

The old warrior nodded and smiled. 'I have, Great One,' he said. 'And now you will have found confirmed what I told you earlier, that this Frank is a fit companion for your son, al-Fuazzem. The Frank knows his falconry, can ride like a Syrian, and has the courage of a young lion. You could not make a better choice, Great One; that is my opinion. It is a sin to waste such courage in a garden when it can be used in the training of a prince.'

Al-Kamil nodded, almost idly, and then, turning to his little son, said gently, 'Will you have this wild Frank for your companion, my dear one?'

Al-Fuazzem clapped his hands with joy and jumped up and down beside his father. Then he ran to Geoffrey and took his hand.

'Yes, father,' he said. 'Yes, a thousand times. This wild Frank shall be my best friend.'

Then, as though in sudden doubt the little prince

turned to Geoffrey and said, 'Will you be my friend, Geoffrey of Beauregard?'

And Geoffrey found himself nodding – agreeing to be the friend of a Saracen, a heathen. . . .

Abu Nazir was smiling now and holding him by the hand; while al-Kamil, the Great One, was shaking his head in mild bewilderment.

'I do not know what the men of the future may say of me,' he protested gently. 'They may decide that I was an enlightened ruler – but,' he added, 'I have a keen suspicion that they will merely write me off as a soft-hearted fool.'

But the little prince was not listening to his father's words. He was already dragging at the rough tunic Geoffrey wore.

'Come, my new friend!' he was shouting, 'Let us go to the armoury and find a sword and a lance for you. Then to the stables. You shall have the pick of the white horses! Whichever one you want!'

At the door the little boy stopped and said, 'You do agree, do you not, Great Father?'

Once again, al-Kamil shrugged his thin shoulders as he said, with his gentlest smile, 'Who am I to argue with the wishes of a prince?'

Outside the door, the young Captain of the guard stood to attention and smiled as Geoffrey passed.

'Some men are born with brains and some with luck,' he said so that the lad should hear. 'I have no doubt which category you come into, Frank!'

Geoffrey stopped and smiled at him. 'And some have both, soldier,' he said lightly. Then he followed the excited little prince along the echoing corridor and out into the sunshine once more.

26. To go A-Riding!

LIFE at Cairo during that winter and the ensuing spring would have been pleasurable, if only Geoffrey could have walked over the little hill beyond the Palace and have seen the tower of Beauregard facing him. That was it – in spite of all the comforts which al-Kamil permitted him, he was still a slave.

Nevertheless, there were compensations – in the form of a white Arab stallion, as fleet as the wind, whose red Spanish leather saddle was decorated with studs of gold; a Damascene sword, with an engraved silver hilt, and a long curling blade chased with Arabic proverbs, the very words of which looked as beautiful as any pictures Geoffrey had seen; a shirt of chain mail, dagged at the edges, the alternate links being of iron and bronze; and a helmet – oh, such a helmet as no French boy ever had, based on an ancient Babylonian pattern, with a tall crest, ear-flaps, and a long backpiece to protect the neck.

Geoffrey loved wearing this finery – especially the red brocade baldric from which his sword swung, for this had been specially made at al-Kamil's command, by one of the Palace sewing-women, and bore Geoffrey's name, in an Arabic translation, stitched in silver wire, along its length.

Alys laughed at her brother as he strode like a Saracen Captain across the courtyard.

'Why, Geoffrey,' she said, 'once you have your helmet on, hiding your hair, no one would take you for anything but a Saracen! Even your skin is Saracen colour, after all the sun we have had!'

Her brother gazed down at her as haughtily as he could and said, in a French which had already taken on an Eastern intonation, 'Why, consider yourself, my girl! If you walked into Beauregard in that robe and in those sandals, they would not only lock you up as an infidel, they would whip you for indecency! Why, I can clearly see your ankles!'

Alys pretended to be cross with him, but could think of no sharper retort than to say, 'Why you even speak French like a Saracen!'

'That is because I spend so much time with the prince,' answered her brother. 'As for you, your French sounds more like dog-Latin than a civilized tongue. That comes of your endless reading of Ovid and Virgil, no doubt! I am glad I lacked any talent in that direction! Hunting and jousting are much more to my taste.'

Alys made a face at him. 'You boys have all the luck!' she said. 'Look at your finery! Look at that helmet! Oh, do let me try it on!'

Abu Nazir came round the corner of the white marble building to find the Lady Alys snatching at the shining helmet, and Geoffrey, full of soldierly pride, doing his best to fend her off. The old warrior watched them for a moment, then said laughingly, 'Let your sister try on your helmet, Frank. You should know enough chivalry not to need my advice on such a matter!'

Grumbling, Geoffrey took off the helmet and placed it carefully on his sister's head. She smiled demurely as the thing slipped down. Then her face was completely covered and they all began to laugh.

When the boy had retrieved his headgear once again, Abu Nazir said, 'Now that you have settled your argument, I will give you the message with which my master has entrusted me. It is time, he thinks, that the little prince had instruction in the arts of falconry – and who better for that purpose than Geoffrey of Beauregard?'

Geoffrey's eyes lit with joy; but Alys stamped her foot with rage.

'Once more,' she said, 'my brother has all the luck! He does not deserve it! Why should he ride out, all *grand seigneur*, while Brother Gerard and I must sit indoors with our noses stuck in some mouldering old Latin books? It is not fair; we can ride every bit as well as Geoffrey can. We were always allowed to join hunting-parties at Beauregard. My father always saw to that. I was even allowed to carry a falcon myself, once!'

Geoffrey laughed, sneeringly. 'Yes,' he said, 'and that bird was never of any use afterwards. She kept taking its hood off to see whether the poor creature was asleep or not!'

Abu Nazir said solemnly, 'She will not be allowed to carry the falcons that my master has bought for his son. They are said to be most delicately trained, and of the utmost ferocity.'

Then, seeing the tears beginning to rise in the girl's eyes, he added quickly, 'But I see no reason why you, and Brother Gerard, who is a good and brave man, should not ride with us to the hunt one day. No doubt we can combine business with pleasure. You can read Ovid out aloud, and make the little prince construe, as we ride along. It will be good for you both, undoubtedly!'

Alys turned from him, and ran towards the black marble colonnade which led to her room angrily crying out, 'Good for me! Always good for me! You treat me like a child! I wish I were back at home – away from you all!'

Geoffrey was about to laugh at what he called his sister's tantrums, when Abu Nazir touched him on the shoulder. 'Go to your sister,' he said, 'and offer her my apologies. Though she is the property of my master, she is also a well-born young woman, and should be treated so.'

As Geoffrey walked to do Abu Nazir's bidding, the man called after him, 'And tell her that when we do go riding, perhaps the day after tomorrow, she too shall enjoy some of the finery she envies in you. I will give orders that something appropriate for the occasion be made for her. The sewing-women have little to occupy their time, it seems, from the laughter I hear when I pass their quarters, and it is proper that our prince's entourage should dress in accordance with their position.'

When Alys heard the news, her tears became those of joy, not sadness.

'Abu Nazir is a wonderful man,' she said. 'Do you know, Geoffrey, I think I like him next to father himself!'

Geoffrey said sternly, 'What of Brother Gerard, sister? Does he not find a place in your affections at all?'

Alys gazed at him with wide eyes. 'But brother,' she replied, 'of course he does. But he is like bread, and air, and water – so close to one's life, that one does not think of him as a mere man.'

Then, roguishly, as Geoffrey turned away, she added, 'Just like you, dear brother!'

But when he ran forward to shake her for such disrespect, she ran as quickly as a deer up the little ladder that led to her bedroom, and banged down the door above him and began to laugh.

Geoffrey shrugged his shoulders in bewilderment, then, telling himself that all girls were either stupid or mad, he strode across the courtyard to the Palace, swaggering a little in his armour, as befitted the companion of a prince, even a little prince.

27. Death in the Hollow

THE hunting-party cantered out through the broad city gates on a clear morning. Silver trumpets sounded their salute as the prince, al-Fuazzem, bowed to left and to right from his high-pommelled saddle, his young face set in the formal smile which he had seen his father adopt on important public occasions.

Half a pace behind, to his right, rode Abu Nazir, now dressed in helmet and light chain mail, over which he wore a sky-blue mantle of silk; to his left rode Geoffrey de Beauregard, who had spent the best part of an hour that morning, polishing his spiked helmet, and who now tried to look as regal and as arrogant as the prince and Abu Nazir combined. Immediately behind them rode a falconer, bearing two velvet-hooded tiercels on a bar supported by a leather thong about his neck so as to leave his hands free to hold the reins.

Alys and Brother Gerard rode in the rear, and a strange contrast they now made. The priest's tonsure no longer existed and his black hair grew out, as stubbly as a gorse-bush, from his head, uncombed and unoiled. His robe, which had long since faded to a dirty grey colour, flapped in tatters about his brown legs as he rode. He looked more like a sturdy beggar, or a common soldier, than a man of God.

But Alys looked more like a princess than anything else. Her thick golden hair had been plaited and coiled within a thin circlet of gold; beneath a short jacket of cloth of gold, she wore a tunic of blue samite, embroidered with silver thread at the hem and glistening with a myriad sequins. Red leather buskins, of best Moorish work, reached to her knees. Her silver spurs had rowels inlaid with many-coloured enamels. On her arms she wore torques of dark gold, turned and twisted in the old Celtic manner, and on her finger a broad ring of gold inlaid with ivory. Only the leather strap about her throat betrayed the fact that she was a slave, and not a free woman of the noblest family.

Before they had set out, Abu Nazir had ridden up to her and whispered, 'Al-Kamil, who admires you as though you were his own daughter, gives you permission to take off your slave's collar when you ride with the prince in public.'

Alys had looked back at him and said, 'And must I put on my collar again, like a dog, when I return to the Palace?'

Abu Nazir had stared away, across the courtyard. 'I am afraid so,' he had answered. 'That is the custom.'

'Then I would rather keep it on, Abu Nazir,' the girl had said. 'I am no lover of games of make-believe. If I am a slave, what matter who knows it?'

But Geoffrey had no scruples about slipping off his collar, for he was proud in a different way from his sister.

And so the party cantered away from the city, and out into the freshly growing countryside. Before mid-morning they had set the tiercels at six brace of pigeons, which the falconer now carried, slung in a net at his pony's side. With each kill, the little prince had bobbed up and down in the saddle, clapping his bejewelled hands. But Brother Gerard had looked away, his eyes focused on the far distance, in disapproval.

At midday the party halted, in the shade of a grove of trees, to eat and drink. The little prince would have eaten nothing but figs and dates, crystallized in sugar, but Abu Nazir insisted that he should add good wheaten bread and goat's milk cheese to his diet. They all drank sherbet, and a concoction of citrus fruits, flavoured with cinnamon. Geoffrey, who had been brought up to drink mead, or red wine, or rough Norman cider, like all other boys of his class, at first scorned these Saracen beverages. But now, after six months at the court of al-Kamil, he accepted them gladly.

As they sat in the shade of the cedar grove, Abu Nazir said gravely to Brother Gerard, 'Yours is not the only tragedy, priest. We have heard that the children of half

Germany, led by a crazy lad, Nicholas, also attempted what they called a Crusade late last year. Many of them perished on the mountains, many of them died of hunger by the roadside, before your Pope commanded the rest to return to their homes. No doubt our slave markets will once more profit by this wave of madness, which seems to sweep the Christian world from time to time.'

Brother Gerard bit his lower lip, restraining the reply which he had been about to make. Then at last he said, 'No doubt such rogues as Hugh and William of Marseilles will share the profit with your own slave-traders.'

Abu Nazir smiled bitterly. 'No doubt,' he said, 'for there are rogues in every country. But I can tell you this, Hugh and William will never profit by their roguery again. They swing from the highest gibbet in Marseilles for their kidnapping tricks.'

The priest said, 'God be praised that they got their deserts. Yet that will not help the thousands of innocents who waste away as slaves or lie drowned at the bottom of the sea!'

'Those who have come into Egypt, under al-Kamil, have been well-treated,' answered Abu Nazir. 'They number about seven hundred. That is a small enough number, I am aware; yet it is something to be thankful for.'

Alys burst out, 'But how many of that seven hundred will ever see their homes and families again?'

Abu Nazir answered tenderly, 'Very few indeed, I would imagine, lady. Who would pay the amount of money needed to set them free? Not the Kings of your fine crusading kingdoms; not the Pope, who needs all the wealth he can gather, to pay for yet another hopeless expedition; and not the parents of these poor innocents, as you call them, priest, for they have no money at all, and, if they had, do not know where their children are, whether they are alive or dead.'

Suddenly the little prince clapped his hands, demanding silence.

'I think you are all fools!' he cried. 'All except my friend, Geoffrey de Beauregard! Come, friend Geoffrey, let us ride

away and leave these gossiping old women to their tales of sadness!'

As the two boys swung into the saddle, Abu Nazir called after them, 'Go on, then! We will give you a good start – and still catch you before you reach the red rock shaped like a Frankish helmet!'

Laughing, the two boys spurred away, their hair flying in the wind. Abu Nazir slowly mounted his fast horse and called on Alys and Brother Gerard to join him in the chase.

Geoffrey revelled now in the speed of his white stallion. Little al-Fuàzzem shouted with glee. The stony ground and sparse green vegetation seemed to flash beneath them. The dust rose in spurts from their horses' hooves, to be caught in the wind and flung backwards into the faces of their shouting pursuers.

'Ride faster! Ride faster, you boys!' yelled Alys, forget-

ting to act the great lady all of a sudden. 'We shall catch you!'

'Faster! Faster!' called Brother Gerard, his black mop of hair more tousled than ever.

'Hurry! Hurry! We are on your tail!' shouted Abu Nazir, feeling the thrill of the charge once more, after so many years.

The two boys kicked their heels into their horses' flanks. Geoffrey rose in the stirrups and, glancing back, called, 'Haro! Haro! Haro! Who catches me may take my head!'

It was an old Norman saying he had used many times when he was racing the other lads, back at Beauregard. Some said that it went back to the old savage days, when the Northmen rode across France, pillaging. At that moment, Geoffrey didn't care where the saying had come from; he was far too excited to think of things like that!

Even the little prince was shouting, 'Haro! Haro! Haro!' in imitation of his older companion, when the party suddenly plunged into a shallow defile. Loose stones shot from beneath the horses' hooves, as they slithered downwards.

Geoffrey heard high cries of alarm from behind him, but did not know what they signified, until it was too late. From the bottom of the little valley, a dozen men rushed up to meet them. Men with yellow hair and red hair, wearing rusting mail and tattered surcoats. Even as he pulled frantically at the reins, trying to halt his helpless horse, Geoffrey saw that each man wore a faded cross, that had once been red, painted upon his tabard.

'Fly for your lives!' yelled Abu Nazir. 'These are Franks!'

Alys saw their fierce faces, the blood-stained bandages about their foreheads or legs, their cold grey eyes, and she was suddenly afraid; afraid, though they were men of her own religion; perhaps men of her own country.

Then the nightmare began to take its ghastly shape. A burly ruffian with a great red beard clutched at the little prince's bridle. Al-Fuazzem gave a wild cry and slashed down at the man's head. He uttered a shriek and toppled to the ground, to roll on down the slope.

Abu Nazir was beside the prince now, shouting 'Make your way up the slope, Great One. I will hold them back!'

But even as he spoke, a bow-string twanged, and the old Saracen warrior half-rose in his stirrups, then gave a groan and toppled to the ground as heavily as a sack of sand.

Geoffrey heard himself yell out, 'Death to the Infidel!' Then his own sword was out and he was cutting this way and that, swinging his white stallion round and round, trying to defend his sister and the prince at the same time. Four crusaders clustered about him, trying to drag him from the horse. Geoffrey felt the butt of a javelin strike him violently in the side. He bent round and hit out at his assailant and heard the man groan.

Then Alys was beside him, holding a sword. Geoffrey saw that it was al-Fuazzem's weapon.

'Where is the prince?' he gasped.

'He has escaped!' said the girl hoarsely. 'He flung me his sword as he went!'

Then she too began to strike out beside her brother, and with each blow her enemies drew back.

Suddenly the bow-string twanged again, with a noise like the notes of some harp of fury. Geoffrey's white stallion snorted and pawed the air in agony. As the mortally stricken creature whirled about, it brought the girl's pony down at the same time. As Geoffrey rolled clear of the flailing hooves, he saw his sister fall clear of her mount and lie still.

Then Brother Gerard was standing over her, his long sleeve rolled back, the prince's bright blade whirling in his hand, his usually mild eyes aflame with anger.

The priest was still fighting, defending the prostrate girl, when a huge man wearing a bandage over his right eye, leaned over Geoffrey and struck him on the temples with the flat of his broad sword.

The boy gave a despairing groan and the darkness closed in upon his mind!

28. *Captured*

WHEN Geoffrey regained his senses, the sun had begun to sink. His head throbbed with pain and his limbs felt helpless. It was some time before he understood that he was bound, hand and foot, and lying across the back of a horse. By turning his head painfully, he saw that his sister and Brother Gerard were walking beside him, their hands tied behind their backs.

Alys had lost her gold circlet and the rich bracelets, he observed. Then, with a great sense of disappointment and loss, he realized that he had lost his fine helmet and the beautiful shirt of mail.

Geoffrey gave a groan and lapsed once more into unconsciousness.

When he woke again, it was dark, and he was lying beside a fire. Alys and the priest also lay, huddled together, asleep.

The man with the bandage over his eye sat down beside Geoffrey. The boy saw the white, half-healed scars that lined his sun-burned face, and the livid marks across the backs of his hands and forearms – the wounds of a warrior.

In guttural Arabic, the man said slowly, 'I am sorry I was forced to hit you so hard, but in battle one must do as one may. You are a prince, are you not? One whose father would pay a good ransom, let us say? Are you related to al-Kamil, for instance?'

Geoffrey gazed at the man as arrogantly as he could manage. In Arabic he replied, 'I am French. My name is Geoffrey de Beauregard. The other two are my sister, Alys, and our priest, Brother Gerard. If you are a true Christian, as the Cross upon your breast would seem to indicate, then your duty is to set us free. There should be no talk of ransom among Christians.'

The crusader stared back at him, his face clouded with

doubt. As Geoffrey looked up, he saw that a group of other men had gathered round him. One of them, a thin man, whose right arm hung heavily in a rough sling, answered in Arabic, 'He is a liar! He is a Saracen, like the little one, like the old one we killed. That was Abu Nazir, half of Christendom knew him. And Abu Nazir would ride with none but Saracens. We all know that!'

Geoffrey rose in anger. Now he spoke in French. 'You dolts!' he almost shouted. 'I am a good Frenchman and a Christian. Unless you treat us well, you shall suffer, I promise you that!' But the men only stared at him in wonder, their faces puzzled.

Now Brother Gerard was awake.

'What language do you speak?' he asked in Arabic. 'Where do you come from?'

The man with the wounded arm glanced down at the priest, his thin face twisted in a sneer.

'We speak the language of our own country, you fool!' he said. 'We are men of Hungary. We know nothing of French.'

For a while there was a grim silence, broken only by the night breezes which blew across the open tract of land. Then the man with the bandage over his eye said, 'You, who call yourself Geoffrey, have wounded three of us, while the Saracen prince has killed our leader. We are soldiers, we are not priests. We have come from our homes in Hungary to make our fortunes, not to prate about religion. Our comrades have been killed, or wounded, by you; that is good enough for us! We believe you are Saracens – but even if you are what you say, a payment must be made for the damage you have done. You may call it ransom if you will, it makes no matter!'

Geoffrey considered for a moment, then he said in French to Brother Gerard, 'These are hard men, soldiers of fortune. They are quite ruthless. Let us send to al-Kamil. Surely he will help us?'

The priest looked down at the dusty ground as he replied, 'There are two reasons against that, my friend. First, these men are Christians while al-Kamil, kind as he is, is an infidel. It seems unrighteous that we should beg a heathen to assist us against our own kind. Secondly, if we go back to Cairo, you will become slaves once more, whereas if we take what chance God sends us, with these men, you will still be free. That is my opinion.'

Geoffrey nodded. 'Perhaps you are right, Brother Gerard,' he said. 'Yet one might have expected gentler treatment from fellow-Christians.'

The priest smiled cynically. 'Christendom is not only at war with Islam, it is always at war within itself. The Holy Land swarms with such rogues as these. They are no more than robber bands. They set up kingdoms here and there, only for the next swarm to knock them down. It is always the biggest rogue who crowns himself king. They speak half the tongues of the earth – and the only tongue they all understand is that of the heathen they profess to fight, Arabic.'

At this point one of the Hungarians, a short squat man with the wide stare of an idiot, struck the priest across the face. 'Be quiet, you!' he said, in Arabic. 'You talk too much. Let the one who calls himself Geoffrey tell us who will pay your ransom money.'

Geoffrey looked up at the man with narrowed eyes. His jaw was set as he spoke. 'There will be no ransom money, my friend,' he said. 'Nor have you the right to ask it, for we are free Christians, the three of us.'

He was not prepared for the blow which he received in the mouth as soon as he had spoken. Then, as the boy's head sang with the impact of the blow, the man with the bandage over his eye said slowly, 'So be it. We shall take you with us, as long as we have enough food and drink for you. But when that runs out we shall leave you – perhaps in the desert, who knows?'

Geoffrey was about to make some hot-tempered reply to the man, but just then Alys woke from her sleep and he remained silent, so as not to worry her by further quarrelling.

'What do these men say, brother?' she asked sleepily.

Geoffrey turned his face away from the firelight so that she should not see his swollen lips.

'They say they may set us free tomorrow,' he said quietly. 'But we must stay tied up for the time being, until they are sure we mean them no harm.'

The girl smiled and lay down again.

Brother Gerard nodded at Geoffrey as though in approval of what the boy had said.

Then, from sheer exhaustion, they all slept, though the wind which blew upon them from the north had become bitterly cold.

29. *Plan of Escape*

SUDDENLY Geoffrey was awake. The night was dark, the sky above him being a deep indigo. Here and there, in a thousand places, it seemed that tiny holes had been punctured in the sky, and that a bright silvery light was shining behind them. He called to mind a dress his mother had once worn at the Feast of Saint Michel; it had been a deep blue dress of a tightly woven material, slashed here and there, on bodice and sleeves, so as to reveal the tunic of silver thread worn beneath it. . . .

Then his mind focused. He came away from the past and found himself very much in the present; the fire was a heap of dead, white ashes, and he was cold, very cold. Someone was tapping him on the upper arm, rhythmically, as though trying to attract his attention. Puzzled, the boy turned his head to see who was touching him. It was the man with the bandage over his eye.

'Do not make a sound, boy,' he whispered hoarsely. 'All the others are asleep. I would not wish to wake them!'

He smiled grimly in the pale moonlight.

'What do you want?' asked Geoffrey suspiciously.

The man smiled again and moved a little closer, looking round from time to time, as though to make sure that he was not being observed by his comrades.

'I could help you,' he whispered. 'That is, if you wished me to.'

'What do you mean?' asked Geoffrey. 'I do not understand.'

The man said quietly, 'If you stay here, with these others, it is likely that misfortune will befall you. You will either die of starvation, or be sold into slavery to any passing band of Saracens. But if you come with me, perhaps we might have the good fortune to meet a troop of Templars or

Hospitallers, who would take charge of you and even return you to your family.'

Geoffrey considered for a moment.

'And what would you hope to gain by helping my friends and me?' he asked at last.

The man shrugged his shoulders.

'That would depend on your family,' he replied. 'Perhaps your father would see that an appropriate reward was sent to my brother in Hungary. I would be prepared to take the word of a young man of breeding that this would be so.'

Then suddenly he gave a sign of warning and putting on a gruff tone, said aloud, 'Go back to sleep, you young fool! Do you think I am a nursemaid to be wakened whenever you feel like waking me? Go back to sleep!'

Geoffrey was puzzled at first by this change of manner. Then he saw that the crusader who carried his arm in a sling had awakened and was looking in their direction.

Geoffrey closed his eyes and pretended to sleep. In the middle of that subterfuge, sleep overtook him in reality, and when he woke again the sun was shining full in his face. His arms were numb and hardly seemed to belong to him.

While the boy was still in the process of recalling, with amazement, the conversation he had had during the night, the man with the bandaged eye swaggered up to him, holding a bowl of warm broth in his hands. He held the bowl to Geoffrey's lips.

'Drink this,' he said, a little more kindly, 'and don't forget what I told you. Perhaps the chance may come tonight.'

Geoffrey nodded but said aloud, 'I cannot drink alone. My sister and my friend, the priest, must also be fed.'

The man smiled, showing his broken teeth, and said, 'Have no fear, young one; they will be fed, as well as we are able to feed them.'

Then, after they had all broken their fast, the party set off once more, travelling north, with the sun on their right hand. Now, the three prisoners were untied, but loosely roped together. They all walked, while their captors rode.

Once, towards midday, the man who carried his arm in a sling, called out a warning and led them into a shallow basin, where the men dismounted from their horses and hid behind rocks.

Geoffrey and Alys were about to ask what was happening, but the man with the bandaged eye turned on them a look so fiercely cruel that they were silent, and lay on the ground like the others, beside Brother Gerard.

Soon they became aware of the drumming of hooves, which came so close to the lip of the stony basin in which they hid that the very ground seemed to shake. The crusaders stared at each other grimly, their hands clenched with anxiety upon the hilt of sword, the haft of dagger, the shaft of javelin. The children were aware that the air had suddenly grown oppressive with tension.

Then, just as suddenly, the heavy hoof-beats died away to silence. The man whose arm hung in a blood-stained sling wiped his red forehead and blew out his cheeks.

'That was a narrow escape,' he said, smiling twistedly as he addressed the children. 'A narrow escape – for us, but not for you! Those were your friends, the Saracens! A troop of al-Kamil's cavalry, no doubt looking for you! The little prince will have told them what happened yesterday, and they will be out looking for vengeance! But, by the grace of God, they will not find it – or you!'

Alys could have wept with disappointment at these words. Geoffrey and the priest clenched their jaws and said nothing. When the man with the bandaged eye winked at Geoffrey secretly, the boy looked away, suddenly hating them all.

Later the party left the basin, and struck off once more, towards the north-east this time. The land over which they travelled had changed. Now, instead of being green here and there because of the presence of small streams and rivulets, it was red-brown and dusty, the surface of the ground being covered with stones. What water stood in the hollows was brackish and covered by a dusty scum. The occasional bushes and trees were stunted and dry, their branches as brittle as tinder. Away to the north-east, almost on the horizon, rose a range of saw-toothed hills, dark in the harsh sunlight. Alys shuddered at the thought of crossing such a desolate place, and suddenly she pictured her father's little castle, set snugly beneath the great green hill of Saint Antoine, among the lush water-meadows where the gentle sweet-smelling cattle grazed, and the stout oaks flung their broad shadows across the land for anyone to shelter in.

She looked at her brother, meaning to remind him too of their home and the countryside they loved; but he was trudging on, his face pale, his jaw set, as though he was locked up in some secret thoughts which must not be disturbed. And when she turned towards Brother Gerard, she saw that he also had the look she had seen on Geoffrey's face.

Then Alys felt quite alone, and for a moment or two, thought that she would burst into tears.

Late that night, they reached the jagged hills, and there the party halted. In a cleft in the brown rocks, the ragged band of crusaders built a fire, feeding it with the dry and dusty brushwood which grew there.

The children and the priest were given flour-meal mixed to a paste with water, which they washed down with difficulty with a mouthful of raw red wine, drunk from a rancid-smelling goatskin flask.

'Oh, why are they bringing us here?' sobbed Alys. 'What, in heaven's name, do they mean to do to us?'

Brother Gerard gazed wordlessly at her, then took her hands in his and tried to comfort her.

Geoffrey moved nearer to her and whispered, 'All may yet be well, little sister. The one with the bandaged eye is going to help us to get away – perhaps even tonight.'

Alys stared back at him, her eyes wide, her mouth half-open as she began to phrase her next question.

But Geoffrey put his finger over her lips.

"Quiet,' he said. 'You must not say a word – but be prepared when the time comes!'

Somewhere above them in the craggy hills, a creature began to howl; then another, and another, until the night air seemed full of tormented wailing.

Even the roughest of the Hungarians huddled nearer the fire, flinging more brushwood on to the blaze, to drive away the prowling creatures of the night.

Alys saw that Brother Gerard was kneeling now, his hands pressed together, his lips moving in silent prayer. 'Oh, Geoffrey,' she whispered, 'do you think that we can ever escape from this terrible place and these terrible men?'

The boy forced himself to grin back at her.

'Why, yes, little one,' he said, as gaily as he could. 'I'll wager my tiercel, back at home, against your best pony we do.'

His sister's eyes began to fill with tears again.

'If we could be back home this very minute,' she said, 'I'd give you the pony, and gladly – without a wager!'

30. *The Dream of Gerard*

GEOFFREY would have won his bet. When the men lay sleeping about the fire, wrapped in their tattered cloaks, the crusader with the bandaged eye crept over to him, signalling him to be silent. Then with three quick slashes of his broad-bladed knife, the man severed the rope which bound the captives together.

'Come,' he said. 'Tread lightly and tell your sister to keep her tongue still. The others are sound asleep. Try not to roll the loose stones down upon them as we climb.'

Geoffrey whispered, 'But we're not going to climb those hills, are we? Cannot we stay on the plain?'

The man replied angrily, 'If we do as you say, they will ride us down; but they cannot follow us up there on horses, and they will not risk losing their precious beasts.'

'But you will lose yours, if you lead us away,' answered the boy.

'Yes,' whispered the man grimly, 'I shall lose my horse. But no doubt I shall be rewarded in another way, eh?'

Geoffrey nodded in the darkness. 'I shall do my best to see that you are,' he said.

'I'm sure you will,' whispered the crusader. 'Now, come on, or it will be too late. Follow me.'

The three rose as silently as ghosts and, keeping close together, began the rocky ascent.

They had not gained the summit of the first slope when a dark figure rose before them from behind a rock. Even in the dim moonlight, the escapers saw that it was the dark man who carried his arm in a sling; but now they saw that he held a drawn sword in his other hand. The moonlight glimmered dully on its broad blade.

'So, Kajalos,' he said, 'you thought to betray us, did you? I suspected as much and that is why I waited for you here.'

The man with the bandage, Kajalos, spoke now in a whining tone. 'I swear I meant no harm,' he said. 'The girl wanted to look across the plain when the moon rose. It was just a childish fancy and I saw no harm in indulging it. I swear it, Captain!'

In the darkness, the other laughed sardonically. 'I shall blow my whistle, Kajalos,' he said, 'and then our comrades will come up here and capture you all!'

But even as he finished speaking, he gave a deep groan, and they heard him fall to the ground. His sword clattered for a few yards over the rocks, and then was still.

The man, Kajalos, laughed grimly. 'He should have known better than threaten me,' he said, in a different voice now. 'He knows how well I can throw a knife, even in the dark. Come now, the luck is with us!'

This time they followed him in horror, stunned by the ruthless disloyalty which would let him murder his friend in cold blood.

Brother Gerard whispered as he ran, 'Should we accept our freedom from such a murderer? Perhaps we should. Perhaps he, even he, is an instrument of God. Who knows? Who knows?'

Kajalos turned suddenly. 'For God's sake, priest, cease your mumbling and put your breath to a better purpose. We have far to go before dawn.'

Dawn found them, blistered and exhausted, their shoes torn to shreds, their legs bruised and bleeding from falling against sharp rocks. As they lay in a narrow, dried-up water-course, deep among the jagged hills, gasping, it seemed to them that their nightmare would never end now.

Kajalos allowed them to rest until the sun rose higher in the sultry sky, then roughly he commanded them to follow him once more, and when Geoffrey protested that his sister's feet were bleeding and that she could not walk, he knocked the boy down with a vicious blow of the fist.

'I have risked my own life to save you,' said Kajalos, 'I have a right to demand your obedience. Do you think it means nothing to me to have killed my own comrade, to have lost my horse? And are not my own feet bleeding?'

Geoffrey picked himself up, his eyes blazing with anger, his fists clenched. But Brother Gerard restrained him, saying, 'In the name of God, my son, do not tempt this man of violence any further. We have seen the lengths to which he will go. Let us be patient.'

The priest spoke in French, so that Kajalos did not understand him; but the Hungarian seemed to sense the general drift of Brother Gerard's words.

'Leave your gabbling, priest!' he said. 'There will be time enough for that later, when we are safe.'

So, for the greater part of the day they stumbled on, their muscles aching, their throats parched, their eyes like balls of fire in their heads. Behind them, jackals howled; above them, in the hot blue sky, kites wheeled and hovered, as though in expectation of some ghastly feast.

That night they lay beside a small spring from which muddy water welled slowly. Kajalos would not build a fire, lest they were pursued by the men he had betrayed.

The children fell into a restless sleep of exhaustion, and lay gasping and twitching beside a boulder.

Brother Gerard watched over them until, involuntarily, he too slept, leaning against the rock, his hands in the attitude of prayer.

Only Kajalos stayed awake, his own eye red-rimmed with watchfulness, his head turning from side to side with each sound that came from the night; his matted hair bristling like that of a wild beast. His knuckles gleamed white as bones as his hand clenched again and again on the haft of his knife.

Towards dawn he heard the clatter of hoof-beats, far down below the plateau on which they rested. He crept to the scarp edge and looked down.

An arrow-flight beneath him, along a broad path, and galloping southwards went a company of horsemen. They wore white cloaks on which were embroidered crosses. Their helmets bore noble crests and they rode with confidence, laughing and jesting, one with the other.

'The Knights Templar!' muttered Kajalos. 'Proud dogs, you are! May the Saracen leave every saddle empty before the day is out!'

As the hoof-beats died away, Brother Gerard stirred and said sleepily, 'Kajalos, I dreamed a strange dream but a moment ago.'

'Oh,' answered the Hungarian, yawning, 'and what was your dream, Bishop? Was it of angels and archangels walking in and out of heaven's gates?'

The priest shook his head simply. 'No,' he said gravely. 'In my dream I saw a great company of horsemen, men of God. I even heard their hoof-beats and the jingling of their harness. And it seemed to me that they were laughing and jesting, one with the other. I knew that, if they saw me, they would rescue us all and take us to some place of safety. So, in my dream, I rose and stood in their path, waving my arms above my head and calling out to them for help.'

Kajalos regarded him strangely, playing with the broad knife.

'Oh,' he said, 'and what happened then, in this splendid dream of yours, dear Bishop?'

Brother Gerard gazed away from him, towards the far horizon.

'Suddenly, in my dream, I realized that they could not see me,' he said, 'although I could see them. They rode through me, each one of them, as though I were made of mist, a spirit or a ghost. And, as they went, laughing and leaving me alone, my heart became so full of sorrow that I awoke with the very pain of it.'

Kajalos thrust his broad knife back into its sheath with a strangely vicious movement. Then he clucked his tongue on the roof of his mouth.

'Hm!' he said, smiling. 'How strange! How very strange!'

31. *The Man in the Black Burnous*

THE end of that ghastly journey came more quickly than the footsore travellers, nourished only by strips of dried goat's flesh and draughts of brackish water, expected.

On the third day, as they stumbled on, half-blind in the glare of the cruel sun, Kajalos stopped and pointed to a narrow winding cleft in the furrowed rocks.

'This is the place,' he said. 'I recognize it by that heap of white bones. That was a pack-mule once. See, its skull still grins down at us, wishing us a good journey and a safe arrival.'

Alys shuddered and turned away her head. They followed him then, among parched and aromatic bushes, down through the declivity, often staggering as the loose stones beneath their feet rolled under them.

By late afternoon they arrived at the edge of a vast plain, largely of sand through which rocks rose here and there, as though from an opaque sea. The air swarmed with flies, which, attracted by the perspiring wanderers, filled the ears of the party with their sustained and monotonous humming. 'Cover your heads,' said Kajalos laconically. 'These creatures carry disease of the eyes with them, and they bite sharply.' Then he led them along the side of the rock-face to the ruins of a mud hut, where he suggested that they sat down and waited.

The place had no roof, and only two cracked and tottering walls were still standing.

'For what reason should we wait here?' asked Geoffrey. 'There are other places, cleaner places, higher up among the rocks if we are to rest.'

Kajalos turned to the lad with a strange smile. 'This is a meeting-place,' he said. 'Here we are most likely to encounter those who will take you on your way.'

Brother Gerard looked up with interest. 'What do you mean?' he asked. 'Crusaders?' Kajalos idly flicked small pebbles from his thumb. He shook his head mysteriously.

'No, not crusaders', he said. 'Other men.' The buzzing of the sand-flies now went on without a break until Alys could have screamed out loud with the dreadful monotony of it all.

Above them, in the flat blue sky, three kites swung round in wide circles, again and again, as though they were interested in the travellers below, most interested.

And when even Geoffrey was at the point of leaping up and running wildly into the stony desert, they all heard the sounds of hooves and of men's feet shuffling in the dust.

Geoffrey leapt up and stared through the window-hole of the crumbling hut. He saw a bent and wizened Arab, wearing a ragged black burnous and a broad belt stuffed with knives. He was seated on an emaciated horse whose body was covered with sores. Behind him trudged four men, wearing filthy turbans about their iron helmets, and clothed in a way that the meanest beggar in France would have despised.

Geoffrey was about to ask Kajalos if this was the party they were waiting for; but the Hungarian silenced him with a wave of the hand, and walked to meet the man on the horse, calling out, 'Hail, Manazah the Chieftain! I have brought Frankish strangers to meet you.'

Alys commented wryly to her brother, 'This man doesn't seem a very important chieftain to me. Look at his sandals, they are tied together with cord.'

Brother Gerard smiled and said, 'We must not judge a man by his outward appearance, especially a man of Arabia Deserta, for they often dress in rags while at home their treasure chambers are stacked high with gold and precious stones. What matters is a man's spirit, not the clothes he wears.'

Geoffrey answered sharply. 'It is my opinion that this man's spirit is as mean as are his clothes.'

'Look at his face and read the truth there,' he went on.

Manazah had ridden his poor horse up to the ruined hut and sat gazing down at them. His was a thin and unprepossessing face. His skin was of a sickly yellow hue, his eyes red-rimmed and bloodshot. A nose as sharp and cruel as a hawk's beak jutted out over a thin and grizzled moustache, which, in its turn, drooped down at either side of his tight-lipped mouth.

'Are they healthy?' he asked Kajalos, waving with a broad gesture towards the friends. 'Are they without fever and sound in limb and eye?'

Kajalos answered him in Arabic. 'Yes, Chieftain,' he said. 'They are as strong as camels. How else could they have crossed the Hills of Death so quickly and with so little to eat and drink?'

Manazah sucked in his mouth and then smiled cynically. 'Perhaps they have picked up an illness during that journey,' he said.

Then suddenly, and in a rasping voice, he said to Geoffrey, 'Boy, roll up your sleeve and let me see your arm! Quick about it! I can't wait all day!'

Geoffrey, unaccustomed to such a tone, at first resented the words of Manazah, and would have refused to turn back his sleeve. But Alys said to him in French, 'Do as he says, for the love of God, brother, or he may not help us.'

So Geoffrey rolled up his sleeve, and even restrained himself as the old man on the horse bent down and pinched the muscles of his arm.

Then Manazah turned away from him and said to Kajalos, 'Very well. So be it.'

The two men went twenty yards or so into the desert and spoke with each other in low tones, so that their words could not be heard by the others. Manazah's followers sat in the dust, their heads bowed, uninterested in what was going on.

Suddenly Manazah gave a short sharp bark of command. His men rose quickly and ran to the ruined hut. To their horror, the children saw that they carried ropes and thongs.

And though Geoffrey and the priest struck out right and left, while Alys kicked and bit, at length their wrists were bound tightly, and, strung together, they were marched behind Manazah's poor horse.

Geoffrey turned to see Kajalos, standing and laughing beside the ruined hut. From hand to hand, the man tossed a round leather bag, which jingled as it fell.

'You treacherous hound' shouted the boy. 'You have betrayed us!'

Kajalos bent and picked up a stone, which he flung carelessly at the boy. It struck him sharply in the back, making him wince.

'That's what you get for not minding your manners when you speak to your betters,' the man called out, laughing unpleasantly. 'See that you do not speak to your master, Manazah, like that. He once flogged a slave to death for rudeness!'

'So,' said Brother Gerard, 'we have jumped out of the frying-pan into the fire. We are slaves again, after our brief spell of freedom, but with an infinitely worse master, it seems.'

Geoffrey commented grimly, 'We have never been free ... not since we left Beauregard.'

The man on the horse half-turned in the saddle. 'I understand your language,' he said bitterly. 'Save your breath for walking, not for talking.'

Then he kicked his horse forward until the three had almost to run, in order to keep up with him.

And when any of them lagged behind, breathless, or sorefooted, one of the guards would strike out with staff or spearbutt, urging them on and on.

Now Alys broke down completely and began to cry. When Geoffrey saw this, his anger was so great that he said, 'Oh, I could kill this wretch on the horse!'

Manazah laughed savagely and, turning abruptly in the

saddle, struck the boy across the face with his riding-thong. 'Keep a still tongue in your head, you Frankish swine,' he said, 'or we must take your tongue away from you when we reach Jedalah.'

After that the captives staggered onwards in silent agony.

PART FIVE

*

32. The Prison at Jedalah

THEY had now lain for three days in the prison cell of Jedalah. Their nights had been filled with dreams of endless walking, their days with the fear of what was to happen to them.

Outside, the air was thick with the many sounds of an Eastern town; flies hummed, donkeys brayed, camels snorted and screamed, outcast dogs howled. By daytime, the streets beyond the cell window resounded with the chatter of market-women and water-vendors; at dawn and sunset, the high nasal sing-song of the Moslem priest hung over the little town like a canopy of sound, as he called the faithful to prayer from a lofty minaret. Then all other human noises ceased.

Whenever the Moslem priest began his high-pitched chant, Brother Gerard crossed himself and began to pray, almost feverishly, in Latin, as though to ward off the evil influence of Islam.

Geoffrey once tried to climb up the cell-window, to look outside, but the aperture was set too high in the wall for him to reach it, try as he might; nor had he the strength now to leap up, as he might once have done, and hang on the window-ledge when he might have drawn himself up.

Alys was now feverish and sick, and could not keep any food down. The thin-faced gaoler, who brought them a wooden platter of broken bread and tough goat's flesh each day, smiled down at her, almost in sympathy, for he had a daughter of his own, he said.

'You have the water-sickness,' he said. 'It attacks those with tender stomachs who dare to drink the water of the hills. Have no fear, you are not bound to die from it. You may well live, if you will only eat something to keep up your strength.'

But now Alys shuddered at the very sight of food – especially such food as they were given. The gaoler shrugged his thin shoulders.

'Well,' he said, 'if you are determined to starve yourself to death, there is nothing I can do. It is the will of Allah; it is kismet, fate!'

And he stumped out of the cell.

There were four others in the cell, boys a little older than Geoffrey, but so ragged, filthy, and verminous, with haggard faces and staring dark eyes, that they might have been of any age and race.

Yet they too were from France; they too had listened to the magic of the voice of Stephen of Cloyes, and had walked the hard road down to Marseilles. They told Geoffrey that they had been shipped from Bougie to Alexandria, and thence brought to Jedalah, where they had lived in the prison through the whole of winter.

'Your sister has the plague,' said one of them. 'We have seen many with the plague since we have been here. It is not the water-sickness such as the stupid gaoler described.'

Geoffrey gazed at the speaker, then at his sister, with something like horror. Then he put his arms about her, to comfort her.

'That is just as well,' said another of the French boys. 'She will assuredly die. And then later, you will die from having touched her. So, you will both escape from this prison.'

Suddenly Geoffrey was furious with these boys, who croaked like ravens, and drew away to the other side of the cell.

'Who are you,' he shouted, 'to prophesy death for my sister? What of yourselves? Think you not that you might die before she does?'

He was so wild that he hardly knew what he was saying. He only wanted to hurt these louts for hurting his sister.

But the pale-faced boy who had spoken first stretched and yawned, and then said with a thin smile, 'We *know* we shall die before she does. She may live for four days with the plague; but we shall all be dead before the priest calls out tonight.'

Brother Gerard gazed anxiously at the boy.

'How *can* you know such a thing as that?' he asked. 'Such things are hidden from the minds of men.'

The boy nodded and smiled. 'Yes, I understand that, Sir priest, but in this case it is different. We all lie here under sentence of death for refusing to become Moslems, and we are to die at sunset, in the market-place.'

Geoffrey said, all in a rush, 'But that is stupid! They are trying to frighten you! They would never *dare* to do it! It is not true!'

The oldest of the French boys, who lay coughing in the shadow of a far corner, laughed cynically.

'Alas, *Mon Seigneur*,' he said, 'it is only too true I can assure you, with all the heart I have left, that they *will* dare to do it; You see, once our company numbered eighteen; now we are only four. This means that fourteen of us are now mortally convinced that these Syrians mean what they say!'

There was silence for a time. Then Brother Gerard said, 'Your faith makes me feel humble. I wish I might be certain that I myself would show such fortitude in your sad position.'

The boy answered, 'We are not saints, priest. It is not because we set Christ above Mahomet that we have refused to accept Islam. Our choice was not as simple as that.'

The priest stared, bewildered, at the lad.

'What are you trying to say, my son?' he asked gently.

The boy turned listlessly away from him.

'We were offered the reward of lifelong imprisonment in this cell if we became Moslems – death, if we insisted on re-maining Christians,' he said. 'And the reward did not seem to justify the hardships involved.'

He paused for a while, then added, 'You see, we have been tormented so long that life no longer holds the magic it once had for us. There is no more to be said.'

He would have sunk back, in his dark corner, into sleep, had not the priest gone forward then.

'Will you all kneel and pray with me, little brothers?' he asked courteously.

Without a word, the wretches knelt and prayed.

Geoffrey, who still supported the weight of his sister's head, could not kneel, but his lips moved in unison with theirs.

An hour later, the cell door was flung open by the gaoler. Two armed guards stood waiting in the narrow corridor, their drawn swords gleaming.

'God be with you, little brothers,' said the priest, holding out his hands towards them.

But they did not take them. Instead, they merely smiled and waved.

'You will not be long after us, my friend,' said the leader of the boys. 'We will keep the door of heaven open for you.'

They did not return, and at sunset the high wailing of the Moslem priest's voice seemed to take on another note – that of terrible warning.

When darkness came, the gaoler entered again, carrying a flickering rushlight. A tall, grey-haired man, wearing a long yellow robe, walked behind him, glaring at the three captives with sharp and glistening eyes.

'Is this the Frankish girl-child?' he asked, in a thin voice.

The gaoler nodded, 'Yes, master, this is the sick girl, Alys,' he answered. 'She cannot keep a bite of food down, nor has done for three days.'

The man in the yellow gown bent over Alys, held her wrist to count her pulse, then, almost brutally, turned back her eyelids and looked carefully into her eyes.

After a while, he said, 'She is not bad-looking – for a Frank. She is sick, true enough; but she will live.'

Then, forcing the neck of a thin green phial between the girl's lips, he said abruptly, 'Drink this, wench!'

Geoffrey and Brother Gerard watched anxiously, as Alys drank. Then she made a wry face, but smiled. A little later she fell asleep, her forehead now cool, her expression relaxed, as though she was at peace.

Geoffrey stepped forward and bowed humbly. 'I thank you, sir,' he said. 'One day, my father, the Lord of Beauregard will send you his thanks and his reward.'

The man in the yellow robe looked down his sharp nose at Geoffrey, as though the boy stank. Then he said, in his high hissing voice, 'I know no Lord of Beauregard, wherever that may be; nor do I want his reward, or any man's reward.'

He turned, with a majestic movement then, towards Brother Gerard. 'You are a grown man,' he said, 'and so may be thought to have discretion – albeit you are a foreigner, a Frank. I shall therefore speak my words to you, and shall expect you to teach these children how they must act.'

The priest bowed his head and said gravely, 'I am listening, sir.'

The man in the yellow gown sniffed with disdain. 'It will be well for you to listen, Frank,' he said, 'for these words will be spoken once only. I offer you your lives, if you will cast off your stupid beliefs and embrace the true faith, Islam. If you do this, no harm shall come to you – though your liberty will be restricted.'

Brother Gerard said meekly, 'And what if we choose to refuse your offer, sir?'

The man clucked with impatience. 'Then I shall know that you Franks are fools,' he said. 'And you will pay the penalty of your foolishness. I need hardly remind you of the fate which has befallen the little fools who left this cell only today.'

He stood for a while, glaring first at Brother Gerard, then at Geoffrey. They met his gaze defiantly and at last his thin lips twisted themselves into a mirthless smile. As he went towards the door, he spoke for the last time to them.

'I shall return later,' he said, 'when you have had time to contemplate the desperate nature of your situation. Then I shall expect to hear your answer. May Allah give you sense enough to choose aright!'

Geoffrey and the priest stared after him, aghast, as he made his dignified way through the door, past the bowing gaoler.

33. Prisoned Birds

THEY sat once more in the darkness, on the dusty straw which was the only comfort of the cell. Outside, the streets were silent now, save for the occasional shuffling of sandalled feet and the distant lowing of cattle.

And as Geoffrey and Brother Gerard sat, their minds whirling with the decision they must make, a woman's voice rose in song, from one of the tall houses across the square outside the prison cell. It was a sweetly plaintive voice, accompanied by some twanging stringed instrument. With a thrill, Geoffrey recognized that this was not an Arab voice, nor were the words Arabic. The woman sang in French, in the dialect of Southern France, of Provence itself, and the words she sang were as familiar to him as bread, baked in the great stone ovens of Beauregard.

> 'On the hills the red deer run;
> The cattle graze across the lea;
> The rider canters in the sun
> Without a thought for me!'

The song went on to tell how a princess was locked up in a high tower, by a cruel step-mother, and like so many of the ballads sung by wandering minstrels, it had a sad ending. In this song, the girl's father was killed while hunting, and the step-mother went away with an officer of the guard, leaving the girl a solitary prisoner. The verses ended:

> 'In this room my spirit weeps,
> Gazes on the moonlit town;
> While below the song-bird sleeps;
> Never more shall I come down!'

In the darkness, Brother Gerard whispered, 'That is a girl of our own country, a prisoner like ourselves, perhaps one who once marched with Stephen of Cloyes.'

Geoffrey shook his head. 'No, not a prisoner like us. Observe, her song is accompanied by the lute. That means that she has certain privileges, perhaps that she is employed as an entertainer in the house of some important slave-owner.'

Brother Gerard nodded, 'Aye,' he said, 'then she is a caged song-bird, imprisoned for ever like the maiden in her song.'

Suddenly Geoffrey said, out of the darkness, 'I have no intention of becoming a song-bird, imprisoned for ever, Brother Gerard.'

The priest did not answer for a while. Then at length he said, 'You will refuse the man in the yellow gown, when he comes later for our answer?'

Geoffrey replied, in a strange whisper, 'I shall not refuse him, because I shall not even speak to him. But God willing, I shall use him!'

For a moment, the priest was afraid that the boy had taken leave of his senses, but at last he dared to ask, 'What do you mean, Geoffrey?'

The boy answered slowly and confidently.

'Desperate cures are needed for desperate diseases, Brother Gerard,' he said, 'and, by all the saints, our disease is desperate enough! If you were willing to play the man of violence tonight, I think we might stand some chance of relieving our situation.'

The priest whispered calmly, 'Tell me what is in your mind, my son.'

Geoffrey answered as calmly. 'You will have noticed that the man in the yellow gown is a person of some importance, but, in spite of his arrogance, he is not a man of great strength or prowess, I would guess. You will have noticed also that, when he enters or departs through this door, that fool of a gaoler makes an obeisance, bowing his head before him, like the subservient dog he is.'

'Yes, yes,' said Brother Gerard, 'but what are you leading up to?'

'Simply this,' answered the boy, 'that at the moment the man in the yellow gown enters, if one of us struck down the gaoler, while the other tackled the old man, we might bind and gag them with strips torn from our clothes and then make our way out of this place, dressed in their apparel.'

For a while there was silence. Then the priest spoke, almost jestingly. 'For a moment,' he said, 'I feared you intended to shed blood. That would not have been my wish – no, not even the blood of the Infidel. But what you suggest is something different. I see no reason why we should not try your plan – even though I do not think it will succeed, for we may be stopped by guards outside, and, in any case, we do not know our way to the coast. Nevertheless, I think it is the duty of every Christian to defend his own life against the heathen. I am with you, Geoffrey, and may God bless our efforts.'

'Amen,' said Geoffrey.

Then they sat back against the wall, to wait.

34. *The Man in the Yellow Gown*

It seemed hours before the outer door, at the far end of the corridor, opened and let a draught of cold air blow beneath the door of the cell in which the prisoners lay.

Alys stirred, then woke. 'Where am I?' she said, her voice sounding stronger now.

'Be quiet, sister,' answered Geoffrey. 'Be still and stay where you are, out of danger. It may be that we shall see Beauregard once more – if only the luck stays with us!'

He heard her gasp with amazement in the darkness, then he had no time to think any more of his sister, for footsteps sounded along the corridor and a thin line of light showed beneath the door.

As the key turned in the lock and the hinges began to creak, Geoffrey pressed himself against the wall at one side, while Brother Gerard waited at the other.

'Strike hard and may God guide your fist!' whispered the priest.

Geoffrey grinned back, his legs beginning to tremble with excitement. Then the door was flung open and the dim light of the taper streamed into the cell.

Even as the man in the yellow gown passed him, Geoffrey stepped forward and smote the gaoler upon the nape of his bowed neck with all his force. The man sank to his knees and then to his face, like a felled ox. His rushlight lay burning on the ground. Inside the cell there were sounds of heavy blows being struck, and of bodies rolling this way and that.

Geoffrey was puzzled by two things; first that the old man in the yellow gown should be so strong, and secondly that he did not shout out for help.

But there was no time for idle speculations of this sort. The boy ran into the cell just as the man in the yellow gown had caught Brother Gerard round the waist and was about to fling him down. The boy struck once again. The shock of the blow jarred back up his arm and almost caused him to cry out in pain.

Then the man in the yellow gown gave a grunt like an enraged bear, but did not fall.

Instead, he swore a frightful oath and swung round to meet his new attacker. Even in the heat of the moment, Geoffrey realized that the language this man had spoken was French, not Arabic.

Moreover, as the man's hood fell back and his features were illumined briefly by the fitful glare of the rushlight, Geoffrey saw, with a start of mingled apprehension and joy, that he was face to face with his father's oldest friend, the warrior, Bertrand de Gisors!

35. A Ship! A Ship!

THE man's clenched fist fell as Geoffrey stepped towards him, his hands held out in greeting. Then his grim face relaxed and he smiled, a rueful smile, as he rubbed the side of his bruised jaw.

'*Splendeur de Dieu!*' he said, 'but you punch like an English blacksmith, *mon ami!*'

At that moment the gaoler began to stir. Geoffrey ran forward and dragged the half-conscious wretch inside the cell. Then, while Brother Gerard held the rushlight, the others stripped, bound, and gagged the man, whose dark eyes were now wide with terror.

'Have no fear, old one,' whispered Bertrand de Gisors, in Arabic, 'you are not seeing a ghost. Your master lies, bound and gagged, as you are, in his own room. He is not hurt, any more than you will be hurt – if you are sensible and lie quietly until we are well out of the way.'

He rolled the gaoler on to a pallet of straw in the darkest corner of the cell.

Then he turned to Alys and, like a courtier greeting his Queen, bowed and kissed her hand.

'Greetings, my Lady Alys,' he said lightly. 'It has taken me long enough to track you down. But, *grâce à Dieu*, I speak Arabic like a Saracen and I have spent most of the years of my wicked life out here in the East. So, by picking up bits of gossip here and there, I have found you. Now, we will go. No one will stop us, for the guards are off duty. I sent them away myself, half an hour ago. They did not look at my face; they only saw this yellow gown, and took it for granted that its customary owner was inside it!'

Geoffrey, now dressed in the dirty robe and turban of the

gaoler, asked anxiously, 'But what will happen, sir, when we are clear of this town? Will there not be a hue and cry to hunt us down again?'

Bertrand de Gisors said gently, 'Outside the walls of Jedalah, in a little water-course, wait a full company of Knights Templar. We shall ride with them, young friend, as far as the coast, which is not more than four leagues away. And there, unless I am much in error, will be waiting a fast ship, which will take us home, with the help of God's good wind!'

Brother Gerard spoke at last. 'A ship?' he said in wonder. 'A ship? How, in God's name, can you provide a ship? I can understand a troop of wandering horsemen, for the desert is full of Frankish adventurers ... but, how a ship?'

Bertrand de Gisors smiled, a dark crafty smile. 'Friend priest,' he said, 'in these strange times a man must find his friends where he may, and his ships where he can. Let me tell you only this – that al-Kamil is an enlightened man, whom I have known in various situations for many years. I can tell you that he is grateful that you saved the life of his little son, al-Fuazzem, that day when you were ambushed. As for me, my only regret is that my old friend and enemy, Abu Nazir, fell that day before the arrow of the Hungarian assassin.'

Then, as they all gazed up at his swarthy smiling face in wonder, he pulled on his yellow hood once more.

'Come, friends,' he said, 'we must be away, or our comrades, the Knights Templar, will be galloping into Jedalah to look for us, and I am a man who hates unnecessary bloodshed!'

So, walking as swiftly and as silently as ghosts, they passed through the cell door and along the corridor, out into the quiet street.

Only once did they speak again before they reached the water-course.

Alys asked suddenly, 'Sieur Bertrand ... has my father ... did my father ...' Then she stopped

The old warrior smiled and patted her gently on the shoulder. 'No, my lady,' he answered, as gravely as he could, 'he did not marry that lady. He was too upset to think of marrying anyone when you left him. The lady in question has now made a good marriage, I understand, with a wealthy merchant of Bordeaux.'

He paused a moment, then said quickly, 'But why should I waste my breath, telling you the news? Let your father do his duty, and tell you himself! No doubt he is aching to do so, as he sits waiting for you in the ship that will take us home.'

Then Alys began to cry, from sheer joy, and Bertrand de Gisors swung her up on to his broad shoulders to carry her.

Geoffrey bit his lips hard, for he felt rather like crying himself. But instead he said, 'I hope no one has been spoiling my tiercel while I have been away, setting her at inferior birds.'

But Brother Gerard only laughed as they loped along.

'There are no inferior birds, my son,' he said. 'They are all God's birds, every one of them.'

And so they reached the water-course, where their friends were waiting for them.

ABOUT THIS BOOK

IN A.D. 1212 a twelve-year-old shepherd boy, called Stephen, from the little town of Cloyes, near Orleans, went to King Philip of France, with a letter which he said came from Christ Himself, bidding Stephen to organize a Crusade.

In spite of the King's disapproval, this strange shepherd boy announced that he would lead a Crusade, of children, to rescue Christendom. He said that the sea would dry up before them, to let them walk safely to the Holy Land.

Such was his confidence and enthusiasm that children from many parts of France flocked to join him, and, in June, at Vendôme, it is said that 30,000 Young Crusaders gathered. So, most of them on foot, and finding food and shelter where they could, these children marched through Tours and Lyons, to Marseilles.

But that summer was unusually hot, and food and water were scarce in the drought. Many of the children died by the wayside, and others turned back and tried to find their way home once more.

When the remainder at last arrived in Marseilles, they found, to their great disappointment, that the sea did not dry up, to let them walk, as Stephen had promised, to the Holy Land.

After a few days, two unscrupulous Merchants (who were later hanged for trying to kidnap Emperor Frederick for the Saracens), called Hugh the Iron and William the Pig, offered to transport the children, free of charge, to Palestine, in seven ships.

A few days out, they ran into storms and two of these ships were wrecked off Sardinia. The rest reached the north coast of Africa, where, at Bougie, in Algeria, the children were sold into slavery.

Some of them were sent on to Egypt, where Frankish

slaves fetched a good price, and here about 700 of them were bought by the Governor of Egypt, al-Kamil, who was interested in European languages and wanted the children as interpreters and secretaries. It is probable that the children who stayed in Egypt led a relatively comfortable life, since al-Kamil was a civilized ruler, who made no attempt to convert his slaves.

But not all of them were so fortunate. It is said that a small company of children were carried as far away as Baghdad, where eighteen of them were put to death for refusing to become Moslems.

In my story, I have taken the liberty of setting this sad incident in an imaginary town, Jedalah, 'not too far from Egypt', since the distance from Cairo to Baghdad would have been too great for my characters to get there in the time at their disposal!

It is alleged that, of all the 'Crusaders' who started out from Marseilles, only one, a young priest, ever returned to France – and that after eighteen years of slavery.

Medieval histories are notorious for their exaggerations; but the one fact that remains, without doubt, is that the Children's Crusade (and there was a smaller German one, too) was a great and pitiful tragedy.

In writing about it, I have tried to be as accurate as I could, without being *too* depressing, I hope! Anyway, I feel that it is a story which should be told. I hope you do, too.

HENRY TREECE